SCOOP OF STORIES

Paul Groves

John Griffin

Nigel Grimshaw

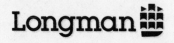
Longman

SCOOP OF
STORIES

Paul Groves
John Griffin
Nigel Grimshaw

Longman

Contents

The Wedding 64

Your wedding day should be the happiest in your life.
But what if it was like Anne-Marie's and Ted's?

Vicky Mills 68

The teachers called her 'insolent'. They did not know
about her home life.

Mr Mobbs and the Strange Power 75

Mr Mobbs was weak on discipline – until he fell down
the stairs.

The Quiet Bully 79

There is more than one way of being a bully.

Hunger 85

You have heard of the Abominable Snowman of the
Himalayas – but there are more frightening creatures
in the bleak Northern waste lands.

The Wee White Ball 89

Mr T Hammenburg, a successful businessman, decides
to master the game of golf.

The Cat that Talked

Old Mrs Tarrant was the nosiest and the most houseproud woman who ever lived. She was bad even before her husband had died – his death was rumoured to have been caused because she would never let him sit still for dusting and polishing – but since, she had got worse. Most of the gossip on the street started with Mrs Tarrant. Some people swore that at the little supermarket they had seen her ears move as she tuned in to what was being said behind the shelves. She could never pass a window without peering in; she could never pass a person in the street without asking a personal question. She took four local papers and if you wanted to know anything about a birth, a marriage or a death you would go to Mrs Tarrant; that is, if you dared for she would soon be cross-questioning you about your new wallpaper or something.

Now Mrs Tarrant had a cat, a fine black moggie she called Felicia. Since the death of her husband she had taken to talking to her cat, telling it any scandal or juicy tit-bit of information she had gleaned that day. At first the cat would walk away, but Mrs Tarrant found that the cat would stay and listen if the television was switched on. Sometimes it even seemed to purr in response. It was quite common for her to spend three or four hours talking to her cat.

One night, during 'Coronation Street', she said to the cat: 'I'm sure Mrs Jenkins at number three wears a wig.' Then a voice said: 'Do you mind not interrupting the programme. You're worse than Hilda Ogden.' Mrs Tarrant jumped for there was no one in the room but herself and the cat. 'Is that you, Mrs Wilson?' she called out, hoping that her neighbour had popped into her hall.

'Don't be stupid, it's me – Felicia – the cat.'

She looked at her cat and saw its mouth opening and shutting as the words came out.

'You're talking!' she exclaimed.

'Of course I'm talking.'

'But how can you talk?'

'Well, you have bent my ears with such a bashing in the last three years with all your rabbitting, it's not surprising is it that I've picked up a few words?'

'I'm all of a shake,' said Mrs Tarrant. 'I must have a gin.'

'Turn over to the big film,' said the cat.

That night Mrs Tarrant lay in bed, all of a quiver. A talking cat! She was in even more of a quiver when an idea came to her. If the cat could talk, it could spy on her neighbours' houses. It could bring her back juicy pieces of information. She did not sleep a wink for the thought of it.

Early next morning she rushed down and gave the house an extra dust and a polish. When Felicia appeared she filled the bowl to overflowing with cat food. Then, filling a saucer with milk, she said in her best wheedling voice: 'Felicia, do you think you could find out if Mrs Jenkins wears a wig?'

'If the grub in this place improved, I might be open to an arrangement.'

'I'll get you chicken cat food, your favourite.'

'I would prefer fresh chicken breasts and some fillet steak,' said the cat, cocking an ear.

Mrs Tarrant rushed out to the butcher.

Felicia was out all day. Mrs Tarrant kept looking out of the window and going out into the garden and calling her. At last, at six o'clock, the cat returned.

Mrs Tarrant was flushed with excitement. 'Well, did you find out? Does she wear a wig?'

The cat seemed in no hurry to communicate. 'A saucer of milk first,' she said.

Mrs Tarrant rushed to the fridge. 'Well?' she asked, as she poured it out hurriedly.

'I can't tell a thing till I have dined,' said the cat. Mrs Tarrant lay out the two fine chicken breasts on a tin plate. 'Do I have to eat off this?' complained the cat.

Mrs Tarrant brought out one of her best dinner service plates. The cat ate slowly. Mrs Tarrant paced up and down in the kitchen.

Finally, the cat licked its paws and sat up. 'Now . . . .' said Mrs Tarrant.

'A little more milk, please,' said the cat.

'But Mrs Jenkins . . . .'

'All in good time.' The cat slowly lapped up the milk.

Mrs Tarrant swept all round it although the kitchen was spotless.

'Right,' said the cat.

'Oh, yes,' said Mrs Tarrant.

'I think we'll go into the lounge. If you could fetch me a cushion.' Mrs Tarrant dashed to get the cushion. 'Not that one. The one with the tassels.'

Mrs Tarrant stopped. 'But that's one of my best. I don't want hairs all over . . . .' she paused.

'Are you insinuating that I'm unclean?' bristled the cat.

'No, but my best cushion . . . . '

'No cushion; no information,' said the cat.

Mrs Tarrant hurried to get it. The cat stuck its claws in it and stretched. Mrs Tarrant stifled a shriek. 'I think I'm ready to begin, if you can sit down and stop fidgeting,' said the cat.

Mrs Tarrant sat down. A great smile came over the cat's face. 'Yes, Mrs Jenkins does wear a wig.'

Mrs Tarrant leapt up. 'Please be calm,' ordered the cat. 'Sit down!' Mrs Tarrant sat down again. 'She takes it off when she has a nap and puts it on a wig stand.'

Mrs Tarrant could hardly breathe for excitement. 'What hair has she got underneath?' she gasped.

'None at all. She is as bald as a coot.'

'Eeh!' screamed Mrs Tarrant.

'Now perhaps you could turn on that quiz show,' said the cat.

Mrs Tarrant fanned herself with the 'TV Times'. 'Tomorrow,' she said, 'you must find out if the marriage at number 10 is breaking up.'

'I might,' said the cat, 'providing there is double cream instead of milk and you do a fillet steak – medium rare.'

Mrs Tarrant paused for a moment. Then catching the eye of the cat she said, 'Certainly.'

Next day Mrs Tarrant cleaned the house from top to bottom. She just could not sit still. At six o'clock the cat returned.

'Well?' asked Mrs Tarrant. 'Are they breaking up?' She put down the double cream.

'I don't see why I should eat off the floor,' said the cat. Mrs Tarrant put it on the table. 'Or in the kitchen.' Mrs Tarrant hurriedly removed the meal to the lounge.

'I think I'll eat on the settee,' said the cat.

'But my best settee . . . .'

'If you object, I'll dine out.'

'No,' said Mrs Tarrant. She carefully lodged the saucer of double cream and the fillet steak on the settee.

3

The cat ate a leisurely meal. Then it said, 'Right.'

'Yes,' said the eager Mrs Tarrant.

'I think I'll have forty winks first.'

'No!'

'It's been a tiring day getting all this information for you.'

Mrs Tarrant furiously dusted all the ornaments in the room. After three quarters of an hour, the cat opened its eyes. Mrs Tarrant stopped dusting and sat on the edge of her chair.

'You will not be surprised to know that they *are* breaking up,' smirked the cat. 'She called him a two-timer, mentioning the blonde from the bakery. He called her a slut and suggested why the milk bill was so low. She threw a jug of milk at him and he blacked her eye.'

'Oh, Felicia.' Mrs Tarrant gave the cat a big hug. This was more than she ever hoped for.

'Do you mind,' said the cat, 'I'll miss "Coronation Street".'

Over the next week the cat discovered that Mrs Foreman drank, that Mr Edwards had a large insurance policy mature, and that Mr Simms had been given the sack for fiddling and had not been made redundant. It was like manna from heaven for Mrs Tarrant. She sang as she hoovered her house daily.

Meanwhile Felicia had put on a few pounds. Then came the argument. It was one night after a meal of fresh salmon. The cat suddenly said, 'I want my boyfriend, Tom, to move in here with a few of our mates.'

'A smelly tomcat!' shrieked Mrs Tarrant.

'Please,' said Felicia, 'you are talking about someone very close to me.'

'And other cats with him?'

'There are just eight of us,' purred Felicia.

'Eight of you!' She could picture the state of her house.

'NO!' she exclaimed. 'What a preposterous idea!'

The cat eyed her. 'No friends: no information.'

'What!' Mrs Tarrant was in a turmoil. She was torn between the cat's scandal-reporting talents and the state of her house. Moreover, if she had eight cats, the neighbours would gossip about her. 'It's blackmail,' she said.

'An ugly word,' said the cat.

Mrs Tarrant's eyes rested on the salmon bone. She played what she thought was her trump card. 'No information: no food,' she said. The cat was too lazy, she thought, to find its own food.

'We will see,' said the cat. It walked slowly to the door and turned its head. 'We will see.'

Later, when Mrs Tarrant was in bed, the cat door opened and in came Felicia, followed by Tom. 'You knock off the phone, Tom, and I'll dial,' she conveyed to him in cat language.

Tom knocked off the phone. Felicia dialled 999.

'What service do you require?'

'An ambulance and a couple of doctors. The old woman who lives here, a Mrs Tarrant, has gone off her head. She imagines her cat is talking to her. If you don't come quickly I think she will get violent and attack me.'

'Your name and address?'

'Felicia Feline, nine Belton Avenue.'

Tom knocked the phone back on. 'I'll get her up in a minute,' said Felicia. 'I'll tell her that burglars are trying to get in.

Mrs Tarrant, in her nightdress, came down the stairs brandishing a large stick she kept for such purposes. She was relieved to hear the siren which she took to be the police. Felicia had told her she had dialled 999. When the doorbell rang, she opened the door quickly. The first ambulance man saw the stick and yelled: 'Mind out, Jim. Quick, doctor!'

The cat was under the skirts of Mrs Tarrant's nightdress. It dug its claws in so that she gave a wild cry. Then it said in a loud voice: 'Clear off, you ugly gorillas, or I'll bash your faces in!'

'She's dangerous, doctor,' said the ambulance man.

'I never said that,' said Mrs Tarrant.

'Who did then?' asked the doctor, coming forward.

'The cat,' said Mrs Tarrant.

'The cat talks then?'

'She has done for weeks.'

The second ambulance man was round behind Mrs Tarrant in a flash. 'Got her!' he said.

'There, there,' said the doctor, stepping forward with a syringe. The struggling Mrs Tarrant was bundled into the ambulance.

As they heard it driving away, Tom conveyed: 'Are you sure that was wise?'

'Wise?' queried Felicia.

'She was your meal ticket. Who is to feed you now? It's either a boring diet of rats and mice or the cats' home. Worse still you could be put down.'

'I don't think so,' purred Felicia. 'I rather fancy a career in television. I think I could run a chat show. We could call it "Le Chat Show". We'll hop on a train to London. I'll teach you to talk. You can be my manager. Come on, say after me: "The cat sat on the mat".'

Igor

'If your uncle Eric sold his house, he could go into a nice home for old people,' said Sharon.

Over the years, uncle Eric had 'lent' them money for a car, central heating, double glazing, hi-fi and video equipment, a new bathroom with a jacussi and holidays abroad. Now Sharon had decided that they needed a new car, some new furniture and the house re-painted. And uncle Eric, who had retired a year ago, had only enough money to live on.

'If he sold his house, he'd have spare money to lend us,' said Russell who always thought more slowly than his wife.

'Go and see him,' she ordered.

Russell went hopefully. In the past it had always been easy to talk uncle Eric into doing what Russell and Sharon wanted.

'Won't sell?' Sharon demanded, when Russell came back.

'He doesn't know how the dog would settle in an old folks' home,' Russell told her. She stared at him.

'What dog? Igor? It's dead.'

'Well – according to him – it is and it isn't,' Russell said.

'What on earth are you talking about?'

Russell explained. Since the death of his wife, ten years before, uncle Eric's faithful companion had been his dog, Igor. Three weeks ago, Igor had died peacefully of old age. Uncle Eric had been heartbroken until he realised the spirit of Igor was still with him.

'He feels its presence in the house. It walks about,' Russell said.

'He's round the twist,' Sharon snapped. 'His mind's gone. He *ought* to be in a home.'

Russell shrugged. It infuriated her.

'You didn't try!' she accused him. 'Ghost dogs! I've never heard anything so ridiculous in my life. I'll go and talk to him.' She flung on her coat, slammed into the car and drove off.

She came back more subdued.

'I can't talk him out of it,' she admitted. 'He's convinced that the dog's still there. He behaved as if . . . . He made my flesh creep.' She shook her head, lost for words.

She wasn't subdued for long. Next night she had a plan. They would send uncle Eric away on holiday. The change of scene would cure him of his fantasies. More importantly, it would give her and Russell a free hand to arrange the sale of uncle Eric's house. If, when he came back, they had an eager buyer for the place, he would fall in with their wishes as he always had done. Russell wondered about this but he knew his wife too well to argue. So he got an overdraft from his bank and booked uncle Eric on a three-week package tour in Tenerife.

Uncle Eric did protest at first. Who would look after Igor while he was away? He was so deeply touched, though, by their amazingly unusual generosity that, when Russell promised to stay in the house to look after Igor's every need, uncle Eric said he would go.

As soon as they had seen him off, they went round to an estate agent and put his house on the market. That night, Russell, who had taken his annual holiday, moved in. That way he would always be on hand for any callers. It would also look, if the estate agent dropped in, as if he owned the house.

He watched telly and drank enough of uncle Eric's whisky to sleep soundly at first, but he was back home at three in the morning.

'You had a nightmare!' Sharon raged at him. 'A grown man! Fancy being frightened by a nightmare.'

'It wasn't a nightmare.' He gazed at her, hollow-eyed. 'When I woke up there was something heavy lying across my legs. I could hear it snuffling. I yelled out, grabbed for the bedside lamp but knocked it over. The weight went off my legs and there was a bump on the floor. Just before I got hold of the light to switch it on, I heard something go padding out of the room and away down the corridor.'

'Rubbish!' she snapped. 'I'll bet you'd been boozing away at his whisky all night before you went up.' He avoided her eyes.

She made him go back. For the rest of the night he sat up in uncle Eric's living room with all the lights on. When dawn came, however, and he hadn't heard or seen anything else unusual, he was ashamed of himself. He put it down to imagination.

He found out how wrong he was when the prospective buyers started to come. The second couple were keen until the woman detected a funny smell. The husband agreed saying it was 'sort of doggy' and he wouldn't like to live with it. The next pair were put off by scratching and worrying sounds which followed them from room to room. Two elderly people attracted by the peace and quiet of the area were driven out by howling and barking which went on outside all the time they were there.

Sharon was forced to take it seriously at last. On the Saturday before uncle Eric was due back, she joined Russell at the house to meet the family who were calling.

The husband was over the moon, as he said, as soon as he got inside. So was his wife. The children didn't say much. After looking through the house, they all ended up in the living room. They were chatting together when the little boy clutched his mother and wailed, 'Mummy! Something sniffed my leg.'

'They're all imagination at that age, aren't they, the little dears?' Sharon put in quickly. It was no use.

'It sniffed me, too, with a hot sniff,' whimpered the little girl and burst into tears.

The mother didn't even notice. She leapt from her seat with bulging eyes.

'Ugh!' she shuddered. 'My hand! It slobbered all over my hand!'

'I can hear it panting,' gasped the husband. 'What is it?'

But they did not wait for explanations and were out of the house in a flash.

Sharon and Russell had to face it. There was no way they were going to sell the house with Igor in it. Russell rang the agent and cancelled the deal. They said nothing to uncle Eric when they picked him up at the airport and he never got to know anything about it.

'That dog – not letting us sell the house,' said Russell when they got home. 'It was defending its master.'

'Anybody could see that,' said Sharon bitterly. 'I don't want to talk about it.'

'My nerves are in rags,' Russell complained.

'You'll get over it,' she told him. 'It won't bother us here.'

But it did. Igor put an invisible but heavy paw in her lap that night as she was watching television. She nearly had a heart attack. It sniffed at Russell in the bathroom in the morning and he cut himself slightly whilst shaving. There were other incidents, including a rather unpleasant one in Russell's car while he was driving to work and another when Sharon was bending to put something in the oven.

'What does it want?' she bleated one evening a week or so later. 'I can't stand it!'

Early next morning she woke Russell by grabbing at him and

crying out. He switched on the light. She was sitting up in bed with wide, shocked eyes. She had had a dream.

'I was on trial,' she whispered. 'There were all these dogs snarling about in wigs and robes. Igor was the judge. It was about the money we've had from uncle Eric over the years.'

'Money?' asked Russell uneasily.

She didn't hear him. Igor's judgement had been that, since uncle Eric was far too good-hearted to want his money back after all that time, they should repay him another way. He enjoyed the sun; he'd loved his stay in Tenerife. In future Sharon and Russell would send him away on holiday abroad twice a year.

'It'd cost a fortune,' Russell gasped.

'Otherwise,' Sharon whispered, 'we shall be haunted even more thoroughly.'

Russell's laugh rang falsely through the bedroom. 'Come, come.' He patted her shoulder. 'A dream. That's all it was. You've just had a silly dream.' She shook her head. 'That's all,' he comforted her. 'You've been worried. We both have.'

It took him longer than that to calm her down but at last, convinced, she snuggled under the covers and he switched off the light.

When something scratched and whuffled and bumped them from under the bed, they almost fought each other to be first down the stairs.

They sat up the rest of the night in the kitchen, drinking tea and agonising over their decision. They hated the idea and didn't tell uncle Eric why they were doing it for fear of Igor. It meant that they had to forget about new cars, new furniture and repainting the house. Russell had to do overtime and Sharon had to take a part-time job in a supermarket. Igor left them alone and a terribly grateful uncle Eric did enjoy his two-week holiday in Tangier that Christmas.

Barratt Holmes' Last Case

It was a wild, wet night off the west coast of Ireland. Breakers crashed against the cliffs. Boats bobbed like corks at anchor. The natives sat huddled over their turf fires drinking poteen. Which is all very interesting but it has nothing to do with our story which is set in foggy London of 1884. Now read on:

It was a real pea-souper that November night. Tomorrow would be a tomato-souper and on Friday it would be oxtail, the flavour of the month. Our hero – Barratt Holmes, the famous detective – stood in the shadows. He knew that his arch enemy, Count One-two-three, could strike at any moment.

'Bong!' He jumped out of his skin. Was that him striking now? No, it was Big Ben. He had just smacked Little Fred in the gob as they came out of the pub. He jumped back into his skin again.

Quickly, he hailed a passing cab. Then he rained it. Then he snowed it.

'Where to, guv?' said the cabby.

'Hush!' said Barratt. 'Walls have ears.'

'They have ice cream and sausages as well,' said the cabby.

'Hush,' breathed Barratt. He put his finger to his mouth. 'Follow that cab!' He put his finger back on his hand.

They dashed off at great speed. Barratt paused only to collect horse manure for his rhubarb. They soon lost the Count in the enveloping fog, and they became – wait for it – stationery.

'Can't you go any faster?' demanded Barratt.

'Only if I carry the horse,' said the cabby.

'Do that then, man. Get me to the Greek Urn at once.'

'What's the Greek Urn?' asked the cabby.

'About a hundred quid a week,' said Barratt.

'I don't wish to know that.'

'Hurry, man! To the Greek Urn. I plan to meet my assistant at that joint because there could be a carve-up.' (Those of you who can see both parts of this joke should write your answer, in Greek, on a postcard and send it to 'Blue Peter'.)

The cabby leapt out of his seat. It was a world record for seat-leaping. He'd dropped his fag down his trousers! He picked up the horse and galloped off into the night. It was a pity for Barratt that he left the cab behind.

Barratt got out and turned down a gloomy alleyway. Then he turned down his trouser bottoms – then an offer to star in the movie of this story. He must catch Count One-two-three because the whole mystery now added up. (Six, we make it.) He crept along, ears pricked. Yes, he'd got the wrong studs in again.

'Ah! Ow! Oo! Aw! Ee! Yaroo!' went Barratt. What had happened to him? Yes, it was the worst thing possible. He'd stepped in some dog muck. He'd stepped in some dog muck when he needed to show the Count a clean pair of heels.

Suddenly he heard someone calling: 'Fred! Fred!'

'You don't know your lines,' he said to the girl in the doorway. 'I'm Barratt.'

'Barratt,' she said in a soft voice.

A young blonde, five feet tall, stood there. He knew that she was five feet tall because he took off his boots to measure her. Her blue eyes sparkled like diamonds; her lips were scarlet as cherries; her cheeks were as red and soft as tomato sauce on a chip butty. She leaned towards him. He let her fingers play in his hair; her elbows play in his ears; and her toes play 'God Save the Queen'. She looked him straight in the eye and said: 'Can I sell you double glazing?'

'That would let in a little light on the case,' said Barratt.

'This case?' She pointed.

A brown suitcase stood on the step. It was crooked because one leg was higher than the other.

'Don't open that!' A small man leapt forward out of the fog. He had on a top hat, a bottom coat, a middle shirt, a pair of halfway-up shoes and custard and jelly coming out of his ears.

'Why have you custard and jelly coming out of your ears?' queried the great detective.

'I'm a trifle deaf. Speak up!' said the man. 'Don't whatever you do open that case!'

'Why not?' yelled Barratt.

'It's got my dirty underwear in it.'

'I see you have a vested interest in this case,' panted Barratt. 'Who are you?'

'I'm your celebrated assistant,' said his assistant. (Author's note: Sorry to keep repeating 'assistant' but we can't remember his name although he plays an important part in the story. Let's call him Gladys. That's a girl's name, you say? Well, why should girls have all the good names? That's sexist.)

'Have you seen that arch villain Count One-two-three?' asked Barratt. 'I didn't recognise you, as you weren't in disguise.'

'He went that away,' said Gladys.

'After him!' shouted Barratt.

'He can't have gone far,' said the blonde.

'Why not?' asked Barratt.

'I sold him a patio door and it's heavy.'

'That should give us an opening on this case,' said the great man.

'If you open this case I'll scream,' said Gladys.

'I don't mean this case. I mean the case of the missing Greek King.'

'That's hard to say with false teeth,' said Gladys.

'Come!' said Barratt.

They dashed off into the night. There was a clatter of armour as the knight fell over. 'Foiled again,' said Barratt, as he tripped over his sword.

'You want to look where you're bleeding going, mate!' said the knight. 'The cabby has already knocked me down once this evening.'

'Have you seen Count One-two-three?'

'Yes, mate, he's gone to blow up the Post Office Tower.'

'But this is 1884. The Post Office Tower hasn't been built yet. Explain that.'

'I don't know, mate. I somehow got in to this story from the thirteenth century.'

'You shouldn't worry,' said Barratt, 'some of the jokes in it are older than that.'

'That's why the Count's been so cunning,' piped up Gladys. 'If the Tower hasn't been built yet, he won't need so much explosive.'

'You'll make a detective yet, Gladys,' said Barratt.

Just then a busker came up playing a barrel with a bow.

'Why are you playing that barrel with a bow?' asked Barratt.

'I always fiddle my VAT, sir,' said the busker.

'Here's a halfpenny. Run to the Post Office Tower . . . .'

'But it hasn't been built yet.'

'Then run to the plans and play "God Save the Queen".'

'Why "God Save the Queen"?' asked Gladys.

'Don't you see, man, Count One-two-three will have to stand to attention and he can't blow up the Tower.'

'Brilliant, my dear Holmes!' exclaimed Gladys.

At that moment a man came up, wearing blue with silver buttons. He had on a pointed helmet and was carrying a truncheon. A notice on his front said: COPPER. A notice on his back said: FUZZ.

'Are you the famous detective Barratt Holmes, sir?' he enquired.

'That's me,' said Barratt.

'Can you tell me what my occupation is?'

Barratt took out his magnifying glass. 'Goodness!' he exclaimed. 'You have set me a real poser.'

'You can do it, Holmes,' said Gladys.

'Ah, there is dirt in your fingernails. It looks like red Sussex clay. You are a gravedigger and you come from Littlehampton.'

'Wrong. I am the arm of the law and the feet of the law, to say nothing of the elbow of the law, and I arrest you for fraudulently passing off that old joke about a Greek urn as a new joke.'

'It's a fair cop,' said Barratt. 'It is my greatest mistake in a long unblemished career.'

'And I arrest you,' he said, turning to Holmes' assistant, 'for masquerading as a woman.'

'I'll write to my MP,' said Gladys.

'I arrested him this morning, sir, for the same offence.'

'And I arrest that man for fiddling his VAT.'

'All the country's doing it, officer,' said the busker.

'Ah, we're a musical nation, sir. Now I arrest that woman for selling double glazing on a Sunday.'

'I deny it. There's no ice cream on my glass.'

'And I arrest you, Sir Knight, for being an illegal immigrant from the thirteenth century.'

'What do you mean? I was born within the sound of bleeding Bow Bells.'

'Ah, but Bow Bells weren't built in the thirteenth century.'

'Neither was the Post Office Tower built in 1884.'

'Don't start that again. . . .'

Suddenly there was an almighty explosion. The Houses of Parliament rocked. Oxford Street rocked. Elton John rocked. Two windows were shattered in Buckingham Palace. They all dived for cover.

'The Post Office Tower!' yelled Gladys.

'No, it's 3C being let out of school at St Chad's Comprehensive. Can you hear that scream, Gladys? Count One-two-three has been trampled underfoot.' (Authors' note: We didn't want too much violence in this story so we thought it best the Count died a natural death.)

'Right,' said the policeman. 'I must now take you all down to the station. I have to catch the boat train to Ireland to arrest those illegal poteen drinkers on the West coast of Ireland.'

'How did you know that?' asked Barratt. 'You weren't here at the beginning of the story.'

'Ah, Walls have ears, sir.'

EVERYBODY: 'They also have ice cream and sausages as well!'

'But what about the missing Greek King. I must finish my case,' said Barratt.

'Never mind him. Marry me instead,' said the blonde.

'I will,' said Holmes.

They raised twenty two children and lived happily ever after. This is how all good stories should end.

The Tailor

'It stinks,' said the little thick-set man. He bent over the bucket of water he had just drawn from the well and sniffed.

'Everything stinks! It's the weather,' said Monsieur Caton. Angrily he pushed the little man's head in the bucket.

In August 1869 Paris was hot and busy. Monsieur Caton, owner of a small restaurant on the rue Princesse, had neither the time nor the energy to bother with complaints from his employees about the water from his well.

The little man stood up, his sunburnt face dripping with water. Calmly he wiped it on his ragged, red shirt. 'It don't taste too good, either,' he said, licking his lips and screwing up his face.

'Well, see if there's anything in the well, you fool,' shouted Monsieur Caton. He stalked angrily back to his kitchen.

He was chalking up the menu on a large blackboard when the little man found him again. This time the little man was clutching a large, dripping parcel about sixty centimetres long and thirty centimetres wide.

'In the well,' said the little man fiercely. He dumped the parcel on the large table in the centre of the kitchen.

Monsieur Caton inspected the parcel. It was sewn in canvas and, as it dried, was beginning to smell.

'Chuck it away! Quick! It's rotten. It will pollute the kitchen.'

The little man trotted off with the parcel. Monsieur Caton followed him with a knife. His black moustache twitched angrily. Some rival restaurant owner had obviously been trying to damage his business by poisoning his well-water. Well, he would see what the parcel contained. He slashed at the calico with his sharp kitchen knife while the little man looked on, smiling – he had been proved right about the water.

Suddenly his smile changed to a look of horror. Monsieur Caton's knife had uncovered a leg – a human leg, cut off at the

15

knee. The flesh was dark green and black, the toes so bloated that the nails had almost disappeared.

Half an hour later, Inspector Gustave Macé and two assistant policemen arrived at the restaurant. Gustave studied the canvas bag and its revolting contents calmly, ignoring the stream of accusations that the shaken and enraged Monsieur Caton was making.

'Who would think he would stoop so low! He'll do anything for his lousy restaurant. Nobody goes there twice. Now he's ruined me. My name will be in the papers. Who's going to come to a restaurant where there are pieces of humans floating in the water?'

'Who are you talking about?' said Gustave, suddenly turning from his inspection of the leg and facing the excited Caton.

'Joseph Vacher. Owner of that filthy hole he has the cheek to call the Mirabelle Restaurant. Go and arrest him. Two hundred metres up the road.'

Caton waved his fat arm and screwed up his face in an agony of frustrated rage, so that his pointed nose became lost in his huge black moustache.

'And what should I arrest him for, monsieur?' said Gustave quietly.

'For trying to ruin me by . . . .'

'By committing murder and depositing a piece of the body in your well. And what is your evidence that Monsieur Vacher is responsible for murder?'

'Well, I . . . . er . . . .'

Gustave Macé was a small, thin figure. Caton, by contrast, towered over him. Before the small man's quiet stare, Caton mumbled and became uneasy. Well, perhaps he was not saying for sure that Vacher had actually murdered anyone but if . . . .

'Now let's get to our business in a calm, organised way,' said Gustave, when Caton had mumbled to a halt.

Three more canvas parcels were retrieved from the well. They contained two legs and an arm. Gustave watched silently as the small man in the red shirt sliced each open with the skill of a trained chef.

'Are you going to piece together the evidence?' asked Caton with a nervous chuckle, as the fourth parcel was opened.

Gustave ignored him. Suddenly he turned and walked away, leaving his assistants to carry on the search for more pieces of body in the well.

During the next few days, Gustave Macé questioned all the people living on the rue Princesse; none more closely than

Madame Bouvier, a frail, middle-aged lady who lived over Caton's restaurant. She had thin, white hair, a small, birdlike face and black, piercing eyes.

'Nimble fingers and fine eyesight you must need for your trade, madame,' said Gustave, as he sat quietly in the next little room, which even the fierce August sun could not light up through the two small, dirty windows.

'I manage well enough,' said Madame Bouvier suspiciously, her head bent over the grey suit she was sewing with quick movements of her thin, bony fingers.

'Business good?' asked Gustave.

'There's always a demand for a high-class seamstress,' said the woman proudly. She had not looked up from her work.

'Do you take orders from people?'

'Of course, how else do you think . . . .?'

'No, I meant, madame,' said Gustave, 'to establish whether you are employed by the public in general or receive orders from tailors. You don't advertise your services.'

'Don't need to. My work is well known. Yes, I do receive commissions from tailors.'

'Such as the one who called yesterday evening, madame. Pierre Voirbo, I believe he is called.'

'Monsieur Voirbo has been a good customer of mine for some years. He's been very helpful to me. He doesn't need spying on by the likes of you, Inspector.'

The woman was becoming hostile, but Gustave pursued his questioning calmly and quietly.

'Forgive me for saying so, madame, but you are not a robust woman. Living by yourself you must find some of the household tasks rather tiresome.'

'Such as what?' snapped Madame Bouvier. For the first time she looked up at the Inspector, her black eyes staring suspiciously.

'Such as drawing water from the well and carrying it up two flights of steep stairs. You said just now that Pierre Voirbo was very helpful to you. Did he ever help you by fetching water from the well?'

'He did many things to help me whenever he came to bring or collect an order.'

'Including carrying . . . .'

'Yes, he did that. But if you're saying . . . .'

'I'm not saying anything, madame. Thank you for your help. Good day to you.'

The only bright thing about Pierre Voirbo was his watch. It glinted on its golden chain when Pierre took it from his waistcoat pocket after Gustave had been chatting to him for about ten minutes.

'Anything I can do to help you find Désiré, I will most willingly undertake, Inspector. I have been most anxious about him, most anxious. But I'm afraid I have some material to collect and I can spare you only a few more minutes.' Pierre popped the watch back into his waistcoat pocket. Gustave faced him across the long trestle table on which the tailor presumably cut out the materials for his work.

'You reported Monsieur Bodasse missing on the twenty seventh of July, I believe.'

'I thought it was my duty, Inspector,' said Voirbo smugly. 'Désiré Bodasse was one of my oldest friends, well . . . . acquaintances, should I say. I didn't see him much but I cannot understand why he disappeared so suddenly – without at least saying goodbye. He was retired, of course, so he was at liberty to take himself off whenever he felt like it but . . . .'

As Voirbo prattled on about his friend Désiré Bodasse, on the police files as 'missing' for two weeks, Inspector Macé studied both the tailor and his room. Voirbo was a youngish man, about thirty, with black, curly hair and an odd habit of tilting his head to one side as he spoke, as if he had a permanently stiff neck. 'Something to do with his work,' thought Macé. The room was poorly furnished. Apart from the long table at which they sat, there were three uncomfortable-looking chairs, bundles of material and half-finished garments, two large winecasks on a sturdy shelf, a pair of scissors hanging from a nail and a large water jug with a hideous blue pattern that stood in the middle of the table. No sign of any axe or large knife that could perhaps have been used for cutting up a body.

'I wonder if you would be kind enough to give me your professional opinion about these,' Macé suddenly cut into Voirbo's prattle and produced two pieces of canvas from inside his coat. He laid them on the table and pushed them towards Voirbo.

'Eh? Two pieces of canvas. Identical. You don't need an expert tailor to tell you that.'

'No, the stitching, monsieur. The quality of the stitching.'

'Yes, well,' said Voirbo carefully. 'One is very neat and the other is, well . . . . not so neat.'

'In fact would you say that the stitching of canvas is so difficult that it could only be done by an expert – a tailor?'

'Possibly so. But what are you getting at?' Voirbo remained

calm, but his head tilted even more as he screwed up his pale blue eyes to squint at the canvases.

'This one,' said the Inspector, picking up a piece of canvas, 'was stitched by my wife. She is quite an able needlewoman, but she would be the first to admit that her work is far inferior to the craftsman's who did this.' He picked up the other piece of canvas and held it out to Voirbo. The tailor took it calmly and squinted again at the stitches. 'Unfortunately, the expert who stitched the canvas you are holding probably also murdered your friend – acquaintance – Monsieur Bodasse and sewed pieces of him into canvas parcels like the one you are holding.'

'Very interesting,' said Voirbo quietly. Macé thought the tailor's hands shook as he placed the canvas back on the table. 'Now I must be going.' Voirbo took his watch out of his pocket and squinted sideways at its glittering face.

'By all means,' said Macé and rose from the table as Voirbo made to go. Macé was not a careless man, so it was surprising that as he rose his arm caught the water jug. It lay on the table unbroken but its contents swilled over the table and on to the tiled floor.

'I'm so sorry,' said Macé quietly.

'No trouble,' said Voirbo. 'I'll get a cloth.'

'Please don't,' said Macé. 'Let us watch the water.'

The voice was again quiet, but this time more authoritative – so much so that Voirbo did as he was told. The two men stood and solemnly watched the water collect and trickle round the floor until it formed a pool in a hollow in the tiles.

'Now shall I get it up?' said Voirbo and he smiled with yellowing teeth at the Inspector. What a stupid man he seemed to be!

'By all means,' said Macé. 'And when you have wiped up the water, my assistants will lift the tiles underneath it.'

'Whatever for? Are you mad?'

Voirbo had suddenly changed. His voice was steady but his hands definitely shook as he picked up the fallen jug; and there was panic in his eyes.

'Perhaps. Perhaps not. You see, monsieur, I think that your friend Bodasse disappeared when you murdered him. I think you dismembered him on this very table. If I am right there would have been a great quantity of blood. No doubt you have cleaned both the table and the floor most carefully. But where the blood would have settled, in a pool where the water is, it will have seeped through the joints underneath the tiles. I wonder if you cleaned the undersides of the tiles.'

'Do your worst, you stupid little man. You'll prove nothing.' Voirbo's voice shook now – with rage, panic or both. He stood against the wall like a trapped animal as he watched Macé's two assistants carefully chisel out the three tiles on which the water had settled.

'You came prepared,' snarled Voirbo sarcastically.

'Oh, I always do,' said Macé quietly.

Underneath, Macé found what he was looking for. The dark stains were definitely dried blood.

'These are bloodstains, monsieur,' said Macé, holding a tile out towards Voirbo. 'It is Bodasse's blood, is it not?'

'Motive! Motive!' shouted Voirbo. 'Why would I want to kill my friend? He was very helpful to me. I miss him very much.'

'I know he was helpful to you. In fact, another friend of his suggested that he helped you with money – more than once. Perhaps he would not help you enough, so you . . . . er . . . . helped yourself, shall we say?'

Voirbo did not speak. He remained with his back to the wall, his teeth slightly bared, his head tilted. Only his eyes moved. They watched the Inspector and his two assistants as they methodically searched the room. One of the assistants grunted as he pulled out the stopper in the second large winecask. Attached to it was a length of thin wire.

'Getting a ship in a bottle is one thing. Getting a man's head in a wine flask is magician's work,' shouted Voirbo.

'We have already found the head, thank you, monsieur,' said Macé. 'We found it – well, you know perfectly well where we found the head of your friend.'

Macé and his assistant watched as their companion carefully pulled the wire from the cask. Attached to the wire was a tiny box, about fifteen centimetres by five centimetres. Macé took the box and studied it.

'You seem to have several practical skills, Monsieur Voirbo,' he said. 'This is expertly soldered, but no doubt when it has been opened it will contain the securities missing from your friend's flat.'

He turned to face Voirbo and then showed a speed of movement surprising in one so calm and methodical. He ducked away just in time to avoid the slash of Voirbo's scissors as they plunged towards his head.

Voirbo was young and strong. It was several minutes before he was disarmed and captured.

'Perhaps you would like to make a statement, monsieur,' said Macé when Voirbo's struggles had subsided.

'Get this down, monsieur policeman. And get it down quick. Because I'll say no more after I've said this.' Voirbo's blue eyes were wide with rage, his black hair was dishevelled, his face streaked with blood where his own scissors had caught him in the struggle. 'He owed me money. I gave him three weeks to pay. He didn't. He came with a lying excuse. I split his head with an axe. It took an hour to chop him up and hours to sew him into bags. I'd have earned more than his damned securities are worth if I'd spent the time . . . .'

'Take him away. He's mad!' said Macé to his assistants.

With his head tilting and jerking, Voirbo was dragged away. 'That's right, I'm mad. No guillotine for me. Insane, I'll plead and you'll be my witness, Inspector.'

'You're not mad enough to avoid the guillotine, monsieur.'

'You'll never execute me,' shouted Voirbo, as he disappeared down the stairs.

For once Voirbo was right and the Inspector wrong. Voirbo was not even brought to trial. Shortly before his trial was to begin, his jailor entered his cell to find Voirbo on the floor, his head tilted for the last time, the blood not quite congealed on the gaping wound in the throat. It was never discovered how he obtained the razor that lay by his side.

The case was one of the many triumphs of detection for Gustave Macé. Eventually he became chief of the Paris detective force.

The Well-wisher

When Sue came back from the kitchen with the two mugs of coffee, Gary was sitting at the end of the old settee, twisting the loose threads on the arm that Columbus had pulled out when sharpening his claws.

'Don't do that, you'll make it worse!' said Sue.

'Couldn't make it a lot worse, if you ask me,' said Gary sulkily.

'You'd better not let Mum hear you say that. She's had that settee since her wedding day. She likes the roses on it.'

'You can hardly make out they're roses, they've faded that much. Anyway, she can't hear me. She's started to snore.'

'That's Dad, you pig! Mum doesn't snore.'

'Well, she breathes heavy then. I listened when I went to the toilet. One's snorting, the other's wheezing.'

'Well, your Mum snores like a dying donkey.'

'Look, what's up with you? I just said your mum couldn't hear me, that's all.'

'It's what's up with you, not me. You've been sulky all night. Hardly spoke in the film. Now you're sitting scrunched up in the corner looking about as sexy as a coalscuttle. Come on, say your piece.'

'Well, I was wondering,' said Gary, steadily stirring his coffee with a pencil, 'whether we should have a sort of trial separation. I mean we haven't been getting on too well, I mean, have we?'

'Trial separation! You sound like we're married. Who is she?'

'Who's who?'

'The new girl you've got.'

'It's not like that at all. I swear it isn't. I mean, it's just that I think we've been seeing too much of each other. I just want to feel I can choose more where I go. I mean, I see you three nights a week and in school and then there's my football practice on Wednesdays and I'm not getting my work done. We could just be friends for a bit.'

Sue scrunched up her toes, clasped her hands together under her knees and stared hard at Columbus, sitting happily in front of the fire. 'Stay calm, or at least look it,' she thought. She was almost sure it was that smarmy Sally Dixon, that ever-smiling, blonde-haired creature that looked like one of those rotten dolls you won at the fair. But she needed to know for certain.

'Gary, I can't think that after two years you just want to stop so you can do more work. You can work round here if you want. I'm upset, I don't deny that, but more insulted. I mean, if it was another girl I'd understand, those things happen, but just wanting to stop for no reason. It's pretty insulting, you must admit.'

Sue sounded calm; inside she felt as if a spiky animal was doing exercises in her stomach. She looked sideways at Gary. He had resumed his inspection of the loose threads. Sue imagined the wheels clicking away under his thatch of dark, curly hair.

'I suppose I've sort of fancied somebody else these last few weeks. Nothing definite, mind you.'

'Ah well, that explains it. Nobody can help that. It's just natural. Tell me who it is, and I'll tell you if I approve.' Sue managed a smile that didn't come out too badly, considering the rage that was inside.

'Well, if you're sure you'd rather,' said Gary slowly.

'Of course. I feel better now you've given me a reason. Not insulted any more.'

'Well, it's Sally Dixon. In fact, to be honest, I asked if I could see her – you know, to test her reaction. She's a nice girl, Sue. She said she'd like to but wouldn't till she was sure you and me had finished. She said she didn't want to hurt you.'

'Oh, Sally, is it? She is nice. I've often wondered why she hasn't had a steady boyfriend. She seems on such friendly terms with every boy in the school.' Sue stopped herself adding 'and in the county and the whole country if she had a chance,' because she thought even Gary might notice the sarcasm. So that doll-faced tart was going to steal Gary, was she? Well, she'd give her as much trouble as she could.

Sue went over to Gary, put her hands over his ears, bent back his head and kissed him. 'Don't look so sad. I'm disappointed, of course, but not that much. At least you're going off with somebody nice. I don't feel insulted. To tell the truth, I'm relieved. Things have been getting strained between us.'

Ten minutes later, Gary and Sue kissed goodbye. As Sue watched him walk away, she felt almost sorry for him. Poor old Gary. His reports from school always said he was a bright, lively and popular boy. If there were a column called 'understanding girls', he would have been in the 'very dumb' category. Sue didn't blame him; in fact, she loved his innocence. That scheming bitch Sally Dixon was a different matter, though. She would get her – by every foul means possible.

Sue cried for two hours, planned for two more, and fell asleep shortly after four in the morning.

Next day, Sue left school the moment the bell ended the last lesson. She was not surprised at being followed. Sally Dixon had been trying to speak to her all day; Sue had made sure she had not had the opportunity. Gary had been quietly ignoring them both, probably waiting for things to settle down.

'Can I have a word, Sue?' said Sally, as she caught up with her at the edge of the playground.

'A whole library full, if you're going my way,' said Sue, without breaking her stride.

'Well, it's a bit difficult. Only I don't want any trouble. You see, Gary's asked me out and I didn't want to upset you, if . . . . you know,' Sally ended lamely.

'She's probably as innocent as he is,' thought Sue. All Sally had to do was ignore her, yet here she was trying to be 'nice'. One look at the worried blue eyes confirmed this; it was the chance Sue was waiting for.

'You've no need to worry. I've definitely finished with him. He's upset, I know, but he'll get over it, don't worry.'

'Oh, I . . . . when did you finish with him?'

'Last week; didn't he tell you?'

'No, well, what he actually said was that he . . . .'

'Finished with me? Well, he would, I suppose. Anyway, it doesn't matter. Either way, he's yours. I hope you can stand the competition.'

'Oh, what do you mean?'

'I shouldn't say this, but as you've been so nice about it, it's only fair to warn you there's another girl in Hartford.'

Sally said nothing; but she looked suitably unhappy. Sue smiled with pleasure.

'Don't worry, he only sees her twice a month. Still, he must be quite keen – a twenty-mile round trip on his bike.'

'How . . . . how long has he . . . .?'

'Sorry, Sal. I can't hear you. Speak up.'

Sue thought triumphantly: 'She's going to cry.'

Sally's voice was weak and shaking. 'I mean, how long has he been . . . .?'

'I've just got to pay the paper bill,' said Sue. 'It's down here. See you tomorrow. For God's sake, don't upset yourself. He's a real good laugh, Gary. You'll get on well. I think it's because his dad died when he was young. Sent him off the rails a bit.'

Sue trotted happily down the side street; Sally turned miserably back towards school. She had walked almost half a mile in the wrong direction.

Sue knew one thing about Gary that she was almost sure nobody else did. His parents had been divorced six years ago. His father lived by himself in a cottage in Hartford, a village ten miles away. Every alternate Wednesday, Gary told his mum he was going to the Youth Club and instead secretly visited his father. Gary lived in fear that his mum would find out about the visits, because not only she, but the rest of the family, had vowed never to speak to him again.

It had taken a whole year before Gary had trusted Sue enough to tell her where he went. Sue trusted that it would take a long time before he told Sally.

In the next week, Sue took care to be especially pleasant to Sally. She even braced herself to chat to them both when they sat shyly holding hands, like a couple of first years, at Isobel's party. Gary was especially keen to talk; he was relieved at how well Sue had taken their splitting up. Sally had been a bit distant the first two occasions they had been out, but he had put that down to shyness; they were getting along fine now.

Three weeks later, it was Sue's turn to stop Sally on her way home from school.

'You and Gary seem to be getting along fine.'

'Yes, thanks, Sue.'

'So he's even given up what's her name in Hartford, eh? You must have something I never had.'

Sally looked unhappy; Sue thought she was the most hopeless person she knew at hiding her feelings.

'Well, not really, Sue. I sort of wish you hadn't told me about that, but I know you meant it for the best. You see, he's told me he goes to visit his dad in Hartford twice a month. I shouldn't tell anyone, he says, because . . . . well, I know it's not true of course, because of what you've told me but . . . . I thought . . . . you see, as we get on so well, I pretended to believe him. I mean, if it's only twice a month . . . . and I don't want to upset him.'

The weak-headed, snivelling doll! The simple-minded innocent! Sue was so annoyed that for a moment she couldn't speak. She had been looking for signs of strain in Gary's and Sally's relationship as a result of her plan. She had seen none. This was the explanation. It was enough to make you want to break Sally's dolly legs and arms.

'I think you're ever so sensible,' said Sue. 'It's much the best way; try not to let it worry you.' Sue did her best to smile; it came out rather crooked. She hurried home, vowing vengeance.

It took Sue three weeks of careful watching to steal Gary's diary from his bag. At last she managed it, when he had been sent on an errand by the French teacher, although Jane Clark had seen her zipping up the bag.

'Just looking to see whose it was,' she explained. 'It's Gary Bartley's. I'd forgotten he'd been sent out. Better leave it. He'll be back for it.'

Sue studied the diary at home. It was disappointingly boring – a list of homeworks, football practices, interspersed with 'Sally 7 pm', that sort of stuff. Sue thought about adding a few comments in an imitation of Gary's handwriting – 'Becoming bored with S', that sort of thing – but decided it was too risky.

She had two days to wait. On Thursday evening she waylaid Sally. As soon as she saw Sue, Sally looked frightened. She tried to rush away.

'Hang on, Sal. What's the hurry? Look, we've both got problems. I think we can solve them together.'

'What problems?' said Sally timidly.

'Well, one problem, Gary Bartley. I suppose he went to see his dad – ha! ha! – as usual last night.'

'Yes,' whispered Sally.

'Well, not only did he not go to his non-existent dad, he didn't even go to that girl. He came to mine, whingeing for me to take him back. I told him to get lost, of course; he's a hopeless case.'

'I don't believe you,' whispered Sally.

'Suit yourself, dear. He left his diary. I found it behind the settee. Give it him back, if you like.'

Sally took the diary; Sue looked for tears. Instead there was an unaccustomed red glow to the doll-face.

'I'll take the diary, thank you. We know you stole it. Jane Clark told us. You might also like to know I've been with Gary to see his dad. We got on well. If I were you, I'd keep away from Gary. It took me a long time to dissuade him from coming round to strangle you. I don't think many people would object. I felt sorry for you when you and Gary split up. I still feel sorry for you but for a different reason. It can't be pleasant to be so nasty.'

Sally turned and rushed away. Sue managed not to cry until

she reached home. After an hour, she dried her tears, took out her notepaper and wrote:

> Dear Mrs Bartley,
>
> I feel it is my duty to tell you that your son, Gary, visits his father twice a month and tells you he is going to the Youth Club.
>
> Yours sincerely,
> A Well-wisher.

After Sue had walked to the postbox, she felt better.

Burglars

Mr Mundy was not happy. He lived with his widowed niece. Over the last few days, he had argued, reasoned and pleaded with her. It had been no use. She was still going to have a weekend away.

'But what am I going to do left here all by myself?' he asked, when she brought her bag down into the hall.

'Oh, uncle!' she said. 'Stop fussing! I've told you. I've left you meals on plates in the fridge. All you have to do is to heat them up. I'll be back on Sunday evening.'

'Sunday!' he said as if it was a year away. She eyed him narrowly.

'I've asked Lee Yeung to look in,' she told him crisply. 'So you will have some company. You'll be all right.' Ignoring Mr Mundy's question about the milk, she had gone out and driven off.

He mooched through the house in his slippers. All the rooms seemed larger and emptier and lonelier. When he heard the evening paper flop through the letter-box, he pounced on it with relief and took it into the living room for a good, cosy read.

The front page was devoted to a story about all the robberies that had taken place in the area. Mr Mundy read it with bulging eyes. It left him prey to dreadful imaginings.

'All right?' he bitterly echoed his niece's last words. 'Fine thing to say! Selfish woman. What if someone breaks in here? I could be attacked. All right? It isn't all right at all.'

He went round the house again, making sure that all the windows were firmly closed. From an upstairs bedroom he looked down at the street outside. It was growing dark. Except for a cat, the street seemed empty.

'But who knows who might be lurking down there?' he said to himself. 'They could be hiding behind bushes and walls. It's not right to leave me here all on my own. There's a lot of valuable stuff in this house.'

His mind had turned, naturally enough, to his treasures. He went into his bedroom to look them over. He had a photograph of himself in a silver frame. There were two small silver cups he had won at bowls. He had some silver spoons and a silver fruit knife in velvet cases. He even had the little silver mug he had been given at his christening. All these things he kept in his room for safety – except for Wednesday mornings. On Wednesdays, Mr Harris, who came to clean the house, cleaned all these things for him. He stood over him while he did it, pointing out any bits he missed. Being retired, Mr Mundy had plenty of time for things like that.

He went downstairs and checked the front and back doors, putting the keys in his pocket. Outside it was really dark now. To take his mind off things, he got his tea out of the fridge and warmed it up. Then he ate it, shaking his head and sighing.

After it he felt better and he put the television on. The first programme was about some children. They had just entered a darkened room to discover a man, bound and gagged in a corner. The man was making strangled noises through his gag. Mr Mundy quickly switched to another channel. On that a policeman was talking about a bullion robbery. A large quantity of silver had been stolen from a van. Mr Mundy switched off and found himself in the kitchen, facing the washing-up. He had had it in mind to leave it all for his niece when she got back. Now, he felt he very much needed something to do. Running the hot water, squeezing in the washing-up liquid, washing and drying the pots all helped to calm him.

He had almost finished, when he froze. He had heard the gate creak. His hands clenched on the large oven-glass dish he was drying. Then there were soft footsteps on the path outside. With a dim memory of television programmes, Mr Mundy switched off the kitchen light. Then he stood there in the darkness, clutching his dish and trembling slightly; but with faint relief in his heart when he remembered he had safely locked the back door.

Something scratched and rattled in the keyhole. Mr Mundy's mouth fell open hopelessly. They were picking the lock.

The lock clicked back. Slowly the door began to open. A voice mumbled something. How many of them were there?

When the dim shape of a head poked itself round the door, something snapped in Mr Mundy's mind. With the strength of sheer terror, he struck at it with the heavy dish. The dish shattered and the head fell back, groaning and cursing. Mr Mundy slammed the door and leant against it, panting. Then he froze again. Wasn't there something about that voice that he recognised?

'Oh, dear!' he said. He switched on the light and opened the door. Lee Yeung was on his hands and knees near the step, holding his head.

'Oh, dear!' Mr Mundy repeated. 'Sorry, Lee. I didn't know it was you.'

'Sorry?' Lee snarled. He groaned and flooded the air with unprintable language. 'You're a lunatic, Mundy!' he growled. 'A dangerous lunatic. I come round here to see how you're getting on and what do I get?' He staggered to his feet, his voice rising to a screech: 'This!' He pointed to the large red swelling on his forehead. 'I've a good mind to—' He lurched towards Mr Mundy with his fists clenched.

Mr Mundy skipped back through the door and closed it. He could still hear Lee Yeung, though. 'Fine thanks I get for being neighbourly. I come round here quietly so as not to disturb . . . . Ouch! You stupid, old thing! I don't know how I can keep my hands off you.' He groaned again and then at last Mr Mundy heard him stagger off down the path and all was silent.

Cautiously, Mr Mundy opened the back door and looked out. He would not be able to count on Lee's help now, if the house was broken into. His niece must have given Lee a key so that he could get in. Mr Mundy frowned, peering about. Had Lee still got the key? Or had he dropped it on the path? If he had, any thief could pick it up and let himself in. No. The key was in the lock on the outside. Relieved, Mr Mundy went in, re-locked the door and put the key in his pocket.

He went back into the warmth of the living room. Automatically, his hand switched on the television. The screen showed a picture of a man wearing a striped shirt and a small black mask. He had bristly hair and he was holding open a bag labelled 'LOOT'. His mate, similarly dressed, was putting two silver cups into it. The studio audience roared with laughter.

'Tchah!' said Mr Mundy, switching it off. 'Comedy? Call that comedy? I don't call it comedy!'

Nervously, he paced the room. Then his eye fell on the telephone and suddenly all became clear. Why hadn't he thought of it before? He lifted the phone, dialled and, when a voice answered, he gave his name and address in his best voice and said, 'I'd like a police guard on this house over the weekend.'

There was a pause and then the policewoman at the other end said, 'Ah! Why is that, sir?'

'Why?' asked Mr Mundy, a bit put out. 'Well – because I expect to be burgled.'

'I see, sir,' the voice said patiently. 'What makes you expect that?'

'Everything,' snapped Mr Mundy. 'I demand protection. I don't want my trophies pinched.'

'Your what pinched, sir?' said the voice, giving a kind of snigger. That annoyed Mr Mundy.

'I'm talking about my trophies,' he said loudly. 'My trophies are silver. They're very valuable.'

'Of course, sir,' the voice said seriously. 'But we're understaffed at the moment. I'll ask one of our cars to look in. Keep an eye on your place, perhaps.'

'I don't want it just to keep an eye on my place,' said Mr Mundy angrily. 'I want it parked outside. Day and night.'

'Sorry, sir,' said the voice. 'I can't do that unless you'd like to come in and tell us more about it.'

'Disgusting!' Mr Mundy raged. 'What do I pay my rates and taxes for? I'll write to the papers about this!'

'Well, you're quite entitled to do that, sir,' the voice told him. Then there was silence. Mr Mundy looked at the phone, breathing heavily. He could think of nothing else to say, so he simply repeated, 'Disgusting!' and put the phone down.

Then he sat for a while, composing in his head a biting letter to the newspaper. After that, he began to brood again. Maybe, in the darkness outside, burglars were already lurking. Perhaps they were hiding in the garden, waiting to strike. Mr Mundy uttered a faint cry and was immediately ashamed of himself. That brought him to his senses and he began to think. What else could he do? It came to him at last. 'Hiding' – that was it. He would hide his treasures. Then when they broke in, they wouldn't be able to find them. But where? That, too, came to him. He would bury them in the compost heap.

He got a plastic bag, put all his silver in it and tied the top. He thought again. No one must see him hiding the stuff. He smiled cunningly to himself. That was easy. He could make himself almost invisible. Quickly, he changed into black trousers and a navy pullover. In a final flash of inspiration he pulled a dark grey balaclava over his head. He was ready.

With all the lights in the house off, he slipped through the front door, closed it firmly, and tiptoed down the garden path.

He had got only halfway when he stopped, saying, 'Ah!' He had left all his keys and his wallet in his other trousers. He had locked himself out of the house.

He was turning this over in his mind when a blinding light shone on him and a pleased voice said, 'Hello! What have we got

here?' A policeman and a policewoman came from behind the
blinding light. One took him by the arm and said, 'Been doing a
bit of nicking, have we?'

'Getting a bit past this sort of thing, Dad, aren't you?' asked
the other.

Mr Mundy was too surprised to say anything. The bag was
taken from his hands and examined. The policeman passed it to
the policewoman.

'Didn't get much, did he?' he asked. 'Looks like a load of old
junk to me.'

This stung Mr Mundy and he found his voice. 'That's mine,
that is,' he said. 'I live here.'

'Of course,' the policeman said. 'Just what I thought when I
saw you.'

'Quite right,' said the policewoman, 'only—'

'Yes,' said the policeman. '—only we'd had a tip-off that there
might be some breaking and entering going on here tonight. We
were just coming to call and here you were.'

'A minute or two earlier or later and we'd have missed you,'
said the policewoman. 'Funny how some blokes are lucky and
some aren't, isn't it?'

'I was just going to hide that bag in the compost heap,'
Mr Mundy told them.

'Very sensible,' said the policewoman.

'Sort of thing I do myself all the time,' said the policeman.
'Now – let's not stand here all night.'

'But my name's Mundy,' spluttered Mr Mundy. 'I live there.'
He pointed to his house.

'Then you'll have no objection to taking us inside and proving
it, will you?' said the policeman crisply.

'I haven't got a key,' Mr Mundy quavered.

'Check the house, Larry,' said the policewoman, holding
Mr Mundy tightly by the arm. The policeman did so, reporting it
dark and with no one at home.

'But I *am* Mr Mundy,' Mr Mundy cried as they led him to the
car. 'Ask anyone.'

When they got to the station there was a bit of a flap on. All in
all, it took about three quarters of an hour to sort things out. The
only name Mr Mundy could think of at first to confirm his
identity was Lee Yeung's. When they rang, Mrs Yeung answered
the phone. She said the call had disturbed her husband who was
ill in bed and they had no friend called Mundy.

Everything was sorted out in the end and the police drove
Mr Mundy home, even helping him to get back into the house.

That was easier than it might have been. They found a broken back window through which the local burglar had made entry. They also found quite a few things missing, including Mr Mundy's niece's stereo equipment and Mr Mundy's television set.

Day of Judgement

'What's the matter?' David asked.

'Nothing,' Alex said as he parked his bike outside the Youth Hostel in which David and I had stayed. He walked over to where we were waiting with the climbing sacks.

'You seemed to be limping a bit,' David insisted.

'Oh, that!' Alex scoffed. 'Came off the bike last week and twisted my knee. It's fine now.'

'Where are you camping?' David said.

'I'm camped on a farm in Herdsdale.' Alex jerked a thumb at the road. 'About two miles that way.'

He had only glanced at me. All David's attention was on him. I said nothing.

'I thought we'd do a few climbs on the Buttress,' David suggested.

'No.' Alex shook his head. 'We'll go on Corrilan.' He looked at me. 'That is, if—?' He looked questioningly at David. I might have been a coil of rope or some carabiners or any other piece of equipment.

'Bela? No problem,' David said.

'Right.' Alex nodded. 'Shall I run you down one at a time on the bike?'

'Oh, god,' I thought. I could just imagine the way he drove.

'Not with the sacks,' David told him. 'There's a bus down to that pub near Corrilan every hour. One's due in about ten minutes.'

'See you down there then.' Alex went off, waving his hand in the air.

He was quite good-looking but I could see from the way he behaved that he was fond of himself and I didn't much like him. I didn't say that to David, of course. Alex was David's cousin. They had done a lot of climbing together. I wondered, when we were on the bus, whether Alex was a bit jealous of me being David's girlfriend. I felt he had tried to put me down in David's eyes, suggesting that I might not be able to do the climbs on Corrilan. I did have my own doubts about that, as a matter of fact. I had done a bit of climbing before I met David at the local climbing club but I knew I was not as good as either of them. Being a bit nervous made me talkative.

'There are some hard pitches on Corrilan, aren't there?' I asked. I knew there were. I had read the book on the area.

'Mmm,' David agreed. He grinned at me. 'Don't worry about it. You'll do all right. Besides – Alex will do the leading. He won't take us anywhere too hairy. Not getting cold feet, are you?' His grin grew wider.

''Course not!' I snapped. I was suddenly fed up with both of them. 'Show-offs,' I thought. Men! Full of the old machismo!

'He doesn't say much, does he?' I asked quickly, to change the subject.

'What did you expect him to say?' David looked at me.

'Nothing,' I said. 'He's all right.'

It wasn't true. Alex made me uneasy. The moment we met him I had felt, somehow, that I was being tested.

When we got to the pub he was already there, talking to an older climber called Peter. Peter irritated me, too. All he could talk about was accidents. He told a tale about being with someone who got killed in the Alps and someone else who had a bad fall in America. He seemed to be fascinated with danger – and death. What really turned me up was his tale about an accident on a scree run. It got to me all the more because I had seen one when I started to learn to climb. Two lads, also learners, had run down some scree against the instructor's advice. One managed it, leaping and plunging down the shifting stones like a goat. The other had missed his footing and tumbled a good way. He had escaped with a twisted ankle and a lot of bruises. The man in Peter's story had not.

'We saw this chap trying to run down a scree slope,' Peter was saying. 'Out of control. He couldn't stop. Just managing to keep on his feet. There was a big rock in his way. He crashed right into it. When we got to him he was blue.' He drew a finger across his throat.

I got up then. They all stared but David got up too, and said: 'Yes. Time's getting on. It's a fair walk. Right, Alex?'

Alex drank up and we left.

We had the whole of the Corrilan valley to ourselves that afternoon. The Corrilan face is a rock wall with a variety of climbs on it – some severe, some easier. To get up there, you trog up a long grass slope; the final access is by way of scree to a ledge. From the ledge you can get to all the climbs.

I was not too happy about that scree. It was hard work but it did not worry me as we slipped and scrambled to the ledge. It seemed very sheer, though, and you could not take a step without the stones falling away under your feet like loose sand. So I was rather gripped up at the thought of coming down it. I told myself that there would be the three of us looking out for each other so it would be all right.

I forgot about it when we were climbing. We put up a couple of climbs that were tricky but good. Alex led, David seconded and I came last. Alex was as safe as a fly on a wall and gave us confidence. Too much confidence, as it turned out. We were back down on the long ledge after our last climb and it was David who said, 'We've plenty of time. Let's do "Doomsday".'

Alex looked at him doubtfully. 'It's pretty hairy, you know,' he said.

'Ah – come on!' David urged.

'Bela?' Alex looked at me. It was almost the first thing he had said to me all afternoon. I shrugged. After all that tough manly talk earlier, I wasn't going to start pleading girlish fears.

'If you two think it'll go,' I said, 'I'm on.'

'Right then,' Alex agreed. We went to the foot of 'Doomsday', a climb that went up and out of sight. It was cloudy but warm and close. We waited until we had cooled off. By that time the sky had darkened and it looked like rain but it was the climb itself which gave me the slight shivers. It wasn't cold. I took a quick look at the book as Alex started up and David paid out rope. It was some comfort. The first two pitches were the worst. The run to the top after them was easier.

For about six metres the first pitch was not hard going. Then came a sort of chimney. I thought I could handle it. After that came an overhang and beyond that what the book described as 'a series of delicate moves'. Alex got up all right. We saw him disappear over the overhang without too much sweat. In a short while he was taking in rope. We could not see him but we could hear his shouts. David called back, 'That's me' and 'Climbing' and went up too.

I paid out rope and watched. It was not until David was in the chimney that I realised.

'Dave!' I called. 'Where's your hat?'

Stopping, he looked down. 'Ah!' he said. 'Stupid! Down there with my pack. Bring it up, will you, when you come?'

It started to rain then. I could feel the prickle of the light drizzle on my face as I watched David making his way to the overhang. He made hard work of it. He started up and then had to go back. He shouted to Alex for some advice and began to climb again. He moved slowly, struggling. Then he yelled: 'Hold! Alex – hold!' as he peeled off.

As he swung out from the overhang, he fended himself off the rock wall on the other side with both feet; but, as he came back, he could not turn and his hands behind his back could not save him. He cried out. Then I saw him slump on the rope. He hung there, with the rope creaking and his hands moving feebly about. He had hit his head on the overhang.

'Alex!' I yelled. 'Let him down. Lower him. He's knocked out.'

I thought Alex had not heard and I was shouting again when David began to descend. When he reached me, I caught him and laid him down as gently as I could on the ledge. He tried to speak but he was not making any sense. Then his eyes rolled back and he passed out. His breathing sounded really rough.

'Alex!' I yelled again.

I had a few panic moments in which I was shouting for Alex and he wasn't coming as quickly as I thought he should. Alex was securing his belay and he came swooping down the rope at last. He jumped out over the overhang and I heard him swear as he hit it coming back. He slid down the rest and jumped down. He had to leap clear of David and me. As he landed, he cursed again.

'What's up?' I asked.

'Nothing,' he said through clenched teeth. 'My knee. I'll be all right in a tick.'

He was not.

There were two escape routes off the Corrilan Wall. One was at the top of the climb; the other was down the scree run. Even if either of us had been capable of the climb, it would have taken too long. With the way Alex was, we were not going to be able to carry David down the scree. I could not carry him on my own. There was no one else in sight. Anyway, it is not a good thing to start carrying injured people about if you don't know what is the matter with them and you haven't the right equipment. One of us would have to stay with David.

All of this had been going through both our heads as we wrapped David up as warmly as we could and checked that he had no obstruction to his breathing. We got him lying comfortably and Alex said, 'I think he's just concussed. We got him down in time.'

'*Just* concussed!' I snapped.

'I'm sorry,' Alex said.

'You were supposed to be doing the leading,' I snarled. 'You might have known he couldn't make that overhang. And you know nothing about me! Taking us up that!' I glared up at 'Doomsday'.

'I'll go and get help,' he said. He looked shattered.

'How can you?' I raged. 'You can't even stand on that knee. What a flipping shambles this has turned out! I'll have to go.'

'No,' he objected. 'That scree could be too tricky for you. I'll strap this knee up somehow. I'll make it.'

'Don't talk so daft!' I shut him up. 'I'll go. You just look after him.'

I was blazing as I made my way down to the top of the scree and that was lucky. As I looked down, it was like falling off a cliff but I was mad enough at everybody to be desperate. I gave myself no time to think. I ran and leapt and slithered, flailing my arms when I seemed about to fall and keeping my balance. I went flying down too quickly to be really scared and, to tell the truth, I almost enjoyed the last fifty metres.

I was also lucky to find a phone without having to go all the way to the pub. It seemed ages but the mountain rescue team was there in double quick time. Everything went smoothly and they took us all to the local hospital.

We were all examined. There was nothing wrong with me, of course. David was put to bed and Alex had his knee seen to. I sat and waited. Then Alex joined me and we talked in a stiff, broken way until the doctor came. He said that David was all right and would probably be out the following day.

He was sleeping so we could not see him. Alex limped away and left me with the doctor. That niggled me, especially as the doctor had some words to say about wearing protective headgear for climbing. I mean – I had worn my hat.

Alex had gone to order a taxi to get me back to the Hostel. That changed things a bit; though, when he came with me we sat in silence at first. I thought I had been hard on him. In fact, I began to blame myself slightly for what had happened. I could have refused to try 'Doomsday'. If I had not been annoyed at the way the other two had been so 'macho', I should not have let David talk me into it. I should have had more sense.

I was not the only one to feel that way.

'Things like this don't usually happen,' Alex suddenly began. 'I'm usually careful. It was shocking bad judgement. I don't know what I was thinking of, taking us all up "Doomsday".' He paused. 'Too big-headed all round,' he went on as if to himself. 'Who was I trying to impress?'

'Ah – forget it,' I said, though I had not really forgiven either of them because, I suppose, I had not forgiven myself.

He gave a short laugh. 'I watched you going down that scree,' he told me. 'I was scared at first. You could have had a bad fall. Then when I saw you sail down there I could see you'd done it before.'

There was still a small spark of anger in me.

'I've never been down a scree run before in my life until today,' I said.

He did not say another word until we were back at the Hostel. Then he got out with me and held his arms on my shoulders.

'You've got a temper, Bela, you know,' he said and suddenly grinned, 'but you're a great kid all the same,' and he kissed me.

He was clumsy but it was nice. He hobbled back into the taxi at once, as if ashamed of himself and it drove off.

I was speechless. It was almost the most shattering thing that had happened all day.

I thought about it before I went to sleep that night. If his judgement had been poor, my judgement of him had been rotten. He had not been sniffy and looking down his nose at me all day. He had been shy. He liked me.

The Sure Thing

When the news got out there was a tremendous demand for the
kind of pills Auntie Gina had taken. Many drove for miles,
looking for thunderstorms. Others were hitting themselves over
the head with hammers and chunks of wood. Some rigged up
electrical gadgets and gave themselves rather nasty shocks. None
of that worked for anybody but, for a time, the hospitals were full
of them. Apparently, only Auntie Gina was that special kind of
person with a special kind of brain.

You would never have thought it. She was so ordinary. She was
not much to look at, she had no conversation, she never had much
money. In her gambling, she was just as unsuccessful as she was
at anything else; but she was totally happy. The excitement of
picking a horse, a greyhound, eight draws; the placing of the
small bet; the hope and tension while waiting for the result –
such things lit up Auntie Gina's life.

She did not win often. No – that's too strong. She hardly ever
won at all. But those very rare occasions gave Auntie Gina's days
a final sparkle. She might be poor but she was contented.

The virus she picked up changed all that. She felt bad for a
couple of days. Then she felt terrible. So, she took an afternoon off
work and went to see the doctor who gave her a prescription for
some new kind of pills. Auntie Gina got the pills from the
chemist, took two and immediately felt better. Her mind
suddenly cleared. She realised that if she cut across the park, she
had time to get a bet on for the three thirty at Thirsk. She hardly
noticed the weather.

It had been brewing up for a storm all day. When Auntie Gina
was halfway across the park, it broke. Lightning flashed and
thunder rolled. Rain came down like stair rods. Auntie Gina
sheltered for a moment under a tree. That did it.

A bolt of lightning struck. Auntie Gina could never work out
afterwards exactly what had knocked her silly. Was it the

lightning? Or was it the tree branch that the lightning had cut off the tree?

Certainly the branch had hit her on the head. She had had a lump there like a duck's egg. Lightning had definitely hit her, too. She had seen the blinding flash; some of her clothes were singed, too. When she came to her senses though, and picked herself up off the ground, she did not feel too bad. Sopping wet – yes. Dizzy, too. She closed her eyes and pressed her eyelids with a finger and thumb. No. No harm done. She was all right.

Or was she? Yes. What was bothering her was a vision. When she pressed her eyes she saw a horse flashing past a winning post. She saw the colours of the jockey. She even saw the name of the horse and the time of the race. It was not Sloucho the Third who was going to win the three thirty race at Thirsk. It was Whirlaway. She ran all the way to the betting shop and stayed there chewing her fingers until the race came up. Whirlaway won. Auntie Gina pocketed her very unusual winnings and went home with her mind in a whirl.

It didn't fully register with her then. Later, however, she was doing her pools. It was Cup-tie season and picking eight draws was not easy. Would Manchester United hold Spurs to a draw? Could Nottingham break even with Leicester? Questions like this were always a problem for Auntie Gina. She pressed her tired eyes.

There was the vision again! All the following Saturday's matches were written on the darkness behind her closed eyes with their results. Eight of these – all draws – glowed red. Shaking like a leaf, she began to copy these on to the coupon. After three she stopped and gave a slight moan. She had forgotten the rest! She pressed her eyes again. No – there they were. In the end she got them all down correctly and hastened to the postbox.

Of course, she won. Auntie Gina was the only one who had eight draws that week and she cleared nearly three quarters of a million pounds. Then came the trip to London to collect the cheque. The well known television personality, 'Bunny' Chunner, presented the cheque, made a few jokes and asked Auntie Gina how she had done it.

Auntie Gina's mumbles about lightning and pressing her eyes made Bunny look at her strangely. When the producer moved on to another news item, Bunny moved away. The newspapermen who flocked round then were more interested in what Auntie Gina did for a living so that the end of her story was not followed up.

When Auntie Gina won the pools again the next week, people did sit up and take notice. She was catapulted into a harsh glare of publicity. Auntie Gina did not handle it very well. Snapped up by Bunny Chunner for his chat show that week, she blurted out that she had not only won the pools but picked all the winners – and seconds and thirds – at Haydock Park. Bunny and then the news reporters got the full story out of her. Scientists examined her. People everywhere started taking pills and beating themselves over the head and trying to electrocute themselves. None of it did any good and envy made Auntie Gina unpopular.

She was a marked woman, too, of course. Bookmakers barred her. The pools' owners refused to accept any more coupons from her. There was a public outcry about that with some saying that it was only fair and others saying it wasn't. Lawyers clamoured to offer their services to Auntie Gina to fight her case against the betting fraternity. She paid fat fees to a whole pack of them.

Nor was that the worst of it. She was swimming in money and handing it out as well, hand over fist. She bought a Rolls Royce, a big house with a swimming pool, two whole rooms full of hi-fi equipment, gold taps for the bathroom, a jacussi, a sauna – you name it, Auntie Gina bought it. Bought it? Not exactly. People had gone in for the hard sell with Auntie Gina. She had been pressured and she had paid up.

The fact is that Auntie Gina was not really interested in money or what money could buy. What she was interested in was gambling. That was the sad part. All the brightness had gone out of her life. She wrote cheques for all sorts of stuff to get rid of the salespeople. She could not be bothered. She just wanted them to go away. She was very depressed.

Even when a couple of struggling bookmakers offered to take bets from her at massively unfair odds, it was no better. How can you gamble on a sure thing? Where's the excitement? She *knew* she would win. It was dull. She tried placing bets once or twice without pressing her eyes. Then she lost. But that seemed silly. It was like cheating. What was the point of pretending that you didn't know the winner? She stopped betting in the end.

She became a shadow of her former self. She would mooch moodily round her big house, pausing only to sign cheques. She never looked at any of her purchases. They stood about, gathering dust. Very soon she started climbing over the back wall to escape from salespeople and everything into open country. She would amble along there for hours, sighing and groaning from time to time. No one can say what might have become of Auntie Gina, if Maxie Black had not taken an interest.

Maxie was a big-time crook with a smile like a shark and eyes of steel. He called two of his henchmen into his office.

'This Gina McCann woman,' he said. 'We're going to have her.'

'Whaffor?' said Angel.

'She can't put bets on,' Maxie explained. 'We're going to do it for her.'

'You a mate of hers then, boss?' asked Tiny. Maxie looked at him witheringly.

'Her? Do me a favour!' he requested. 'No. We grab her. She tells us the winners. Then we lay our bets.'

'What if she won't tell us the winners?' asked Tiny.

'She will,' said Maxie confidently. He gave them their instructions and they set off.

Their task was not hard. They found Auntie Gina strolling through a field, muttering to herself. Tiny hit her on the head and Angel applied a pad of chloroform to her face.

When Auntie Gina woke up, she found herself tied to a chair in a cellar which smelled strongly of mould. Maxie explained things to her, while Angel swished a black rubber truncheon through the air. Auntie Gina told Maxie she was more than eager to name all the winners on all the race tracks in the country without delay.

Sweating, Auntie Gina started to babble that she needed to press her fingers to her eyes. Maxie cut her short. He had read the papers and seen Auntie Gina on television. He knew about all that. Auntie Gina had better get on with it. Tiny smiled hideously as he released one of her hands and she pressed her closed lids with trembling fingers. And—?

Nothing. Nothing at all. She pressed harder. Still nothing. It came to her in an unusual flash of inspiration. Either the blow on the head or the chloroform, or both, had restored her brain to normal. She had lost the gift. Her mind went blank with the shock.

'Come on! Come on!' Maxie's snarl roused her from stupor.

Now Auntie Gina had been a bit unwise about publicity but she was not altogether lacking in commonsense. She knew better than to admit that she had lost her strange powers. They would not believe her. They would insist on her naming winners. They would persuade her. She knew what that meant. She sweated a bit more.

Desperately playing for time, she asked for a newspaper. Tiny thrust one at her. Auntie Gina made a bit of a performance of reading it and pressing her eyes and frowning, until Maxie lost patience. Auntie Gina quavered out a list of names and Maxie

43

sent Tiny off with a little suitcase to place the bets. Maxie laid out nearly forty thousand pounds that day.

Time passed. Maxie paced up and down, whistling. Angel stared into space, breathing through his mouth. Auntie Gina thought.

Perhaps, she pondered, just this once – all the horses would win. Perhaps she had not really lost the gift and had picked winners without knowing it. Perhaps Tiny would get run over. Perhaps both Maxie and Angel would suddenly have heart attacks. Perhaps . . . .

Her mind ran on like a hamster on a treadwheel. It stopped dead when Tiny came back. Tiny did not need to speak. His face told the full story.

'All of them?' Maxie hissed incredulously.

'All of 'em, boss,' said Tiny. 'They weren't even placed. Not one.'

The veins stood out on Maxie's head. When he could speak again, he gave his orders. Angel and Tiny were about to beat Auntie Gina to a pulp when in rushed the police.

Afterwards, some were surprised that the police had caught up with Maxie so soon; but Auntie Gina was, after all, a public figure and there were a lot of them on the job. Anyway, the cellar was suddenly full of blue uniforms. There was a lot of noise and Maxie and Angel and Tiny were taking a good deal of stick.

Auntie Gina was the centre of attention. Two sergeants were gently untying her hands, three inspectors were helping her to her feet and a constable was brushing her down behind. The noise faded as the crooks were taken away. The sergeants asked Auntie Gina, in voices of concern, how she felt and the inspectors were very eager to run her home.

A superintendent ordered them all to stand back. He took Auntie Gina with him in the back of his chauffeur-driven car. He was most friendly and respectful. He praised Auntie Gina's great courage in being instrumental in bringing a dangerous gang of crooks to justice. He said he had always very much admired the way Auntie Gina handled herself on television; and, by the way, which horse did she see as the winner of the Grand National?

Auntie Gina told him what had happened. The superintendent took some convincing but Auntie Gina managed it and the superintendent was furious. He accused her of false pretences. He said that if they had known that Auntie Gina no longer had the gift there would have been only one constable on the case. He threatened to send Auntie Gina a bill for all the public money involved in setting up the police operation. He made her get out of the car and walk.

As soon as the news was leaked, interest in Auntie Gina died and it did not take her long to run through all her money and possessions and go back to being a punter in only a small way. As soon as she lost the gift, she got back all her old zest for gambling and her interest in life.

She is as poor as she has ever been, now. Bookmakers no longer try to refuse her bets. In fact, they are eager for them. The gift left nothing behind. Auntie Gina finished where she started – like most of her horses. If Auntie Gina bets on a horse, it may not leave the starting gate. It may get tired halfway through a race and take it easy. It may come last; it just might come fourth. Very, very rarely will it win. You can be fairly certain of that. Auntie Gina, however, is thoroughly happy once more and that is a sure thing.

The Well-planned Job

What went wrong? I can't understand it. I mean – me and Bert
had studied things. We'd watched the programmes on telly. And
we'd seen films. Rob a bank? It looked easy.

I'd planned it all out most carefully. Bert would drive the
getaway car. I'm red hot at modelling so I got a plastic kit to
make a model pistol. All we needed were the stocking masks.
There I did strike a bit of a snag. I'd borrowed two pairs of tights
out of our kid's drawer. Then Bert objected. He said it would look
silly to have one stocking leg hanging down your back. He also
said what if you had to swing round quickly? The other leg might
cover your eyes. Then you wouldn't be able to see. People could
spring on you then and overpower you.

I didn't argue. I just went to a shop. The bird in there was
rather nice.

'Can I help you, sir?' she asked, smiling.

'I want a stocking,' I said.

'Any special colour, sir? What size?'

'I'm not worried about the colour,' I told her, 'but it's got to be
big enough to fit over my head.'

'Pardon?' she said.

'It's not for me,' I explained. 'I'm going to wear a pair of tights.
It's for my mate. We want a stocking for rob— . . . . for
something.'

She kept staring at me as she put several packets of stockings
on the counter.

'These are round the sixty five pence mark, sir,' she said.

'But these are pairs of stockings,' I objected.

'Yes, sir,' she said. 'That's how we sell them. In pairs.'

'Couldn't you sell me just one for round thirty p?' I asked.

'I'm afraid I can't split a pair,' she said, and stood gaping at me.

Then I realised it didn't matter. We could cut a pair of tights in
two.

'Never mind,' I told her. 'I've thought of something else.' And I left.

I got a bit niggled with Bert when I tried out my plan. I cut off half the tights and made him wear it. It looked great. There was the foot sticking up on top of his head. His eyes were slitted up under the tight and his nose was all squashed. It was perfect. If I hadn't known it was him, even I wouldn't have recognised him.

'I don't like it,' he moaned. 'Couldn't you get a proper stocking?'

'I've told you,' I said. 'They only sell them in pairs.'

'It smells,' he said. 'It smells musty.'

'I'm getting a bit fed up with you, Bert,' I said. 'Always objecting. You've got to learn to take orders. Who's master-minding this, anyway?'

'You are,' he said.

'That's it, then,' I snapped. 'Go and pinch a car.'

'I'll feel silly walking about the streets with this thing over my head,' he said through his nose and went off to nick a car. I went back to my modelling.

Bert was gone so long that I was staring out of the window, wondering where he was, when he drove up. He parked and got out, looking pleased.

'What are those white splashes all over it?' I asked as he came in.

'Dunno,' he said. 'It could be birds.'

'Where did you get it?'

'Up a back street near the cattle market. Lucky, really. The key was in it.'

'Hmm,' I said. 'Couldn't you have picked a better one in town?'

'I did look but people were staring at me all the time.'

'Pity,' I said. 'And – by the way – you can take that stocking mask off now you're back here.'

When I went out, it turned out better than I'd thought. It was jerky and noisy to drive around. It smoked a lot, too. But with its back seat missing that left plenty of room to pile up the money and we could throw that in quickly through the missing windows, thus saving valuable getaway time. I think it had belonged to a farmer. I was fairly certain it had carried pigs.

Next day we went down to the bank. I found that Bert had been right about wearing the tight. It did interfere with my breathing. I decided I would put mine on as I went into the bank. But I made Bert wear his as we drove down. We stopped outside and a traffic warden came up.

'You can't leave that here,' she said.

'Why not?' I said. 'We're just popping into the bank for a moment.' I was crafty. I didn't tell her why.

'Bank's closed on Saturdays,' she told us. 'What's that your mate's wearing?'

I looked at Bert. He'd pulled his mask round so that his face stuck out of the hole. You could see who he was quite clearly. I felt there was no point in going on – not with the bank being closed, as well.

'Come on,' I snapped. 'Let's get home.'

It was just the same the following day and it made me mad. We couldn't have had a better time for the robbery. There were only a few cars about, plenty of room to park in front of the bank and nobody doing any shopping except for papers. But we had to come home in the end. We waited an hour and the bank still hadn't opened. Bert began to whine and complain about being cold and about the smell in the car. I got sick of it all in the end and told him to drive us back to the house.

Monday was much better – to begin with. By the time we got there the bank was open. It was busy and there was no space to park outside, so Bert went off to park down a side street.

I went in with my two plastic bags from Tesco's and the gun in my pocket, pulling the tights mask over my head. Fortunately, there was no queue.

'Morning,' the clerk greeted me. I slid the paper with the message on across the counter. He studied it. I put the plastic bags on the counter in readiness. He looked up, frowning.

'I'm sorry, sir,' he said, 'but I don't understand this. What does it mean – "Give me your mummy"?'

'It doesn't say that!' I snapped.

'Oh, yes, sir. It says, "I have gum here. Give me your mummy."'

'That's "money", you fool!' I snarled. 'It says, "I have a gun here. Give me your money."'

'Look.' He tried to show me. 'It's "gum" and "mummy".' He read it again. 'Unless—' he said doubtfully, 'you do your "m"s and "n"s and "o"s in a funny way.'

Then Bert put his head round the door. He was still wearing his mask. All the people in the bank turned to stare at him.

'Psst!' he went, jerking his head. 'Psst!' I realised we were wasting time.

'Cut the argument!' I growled at the bank clerk. I pulled out the gun. 'See this? A gun. Hand over the money or you'll be sorry.'

'That's not a real gun,' he said.

'It is! Of course it is!' I hissed.

'No, it isn't. It's plastic. I make models myself. And you've put it together wrong.'

'I haven't!' I raged.

'Yes, you have. The bit that's pointing up should be pointing at me. And you've stuck that bit on the wrong side.' He pointed. 'You can't have read the instructions.'

'Don't talk daft!' I growled, pushing the bags at him under the glass plate. 'Put the money in those or things will go hard with you!'

I could see from his face that that had made him think and we could have got away with it, if the police hadn't come in just then.

That was the blinking traffic warden's doing. Bert had no sooner parked when the warden came up. He ordered Bert to shift the car. Bert tried but he couldn't get it started again. The warden began to give Bert a bit of aggro and Bert gave some back. Then a copper came up. So Bert ran for it to warn me.

One thing led to another. The next I knew was that there were four policemen in the bank. I tried to threaten them with my gun. But one of them just took it off me, dropped it on the floor and trod on it. Smashed it up completely. That really hurt. I mean – all that work I'd put into it.

I don't know. What did go wrong? The only consolation is that being banged up here in the nick should give me plenty of time to work out where I made my mistakes.

Merlin's Brew

Dalip, Gillian, Peter and Liz were on a cycling holiday staying at youth hostels. They were touring the West Country. That afternoon they had stopped at Cadbury Hill, the legendary Camelot of King Arthur. They went up to the top of the mound to see the view and look at the excavations.

'I wonder if King Arthur did live here?' said Dalip.

'Old Jilks said he did,' remarked Gillian.

'Don't remind me of school,' grunted Peter.

'But just think the knights of King Arthur may have stood where we are, looking out over the country.'

'And Guinevere at King Arthur's side,' added Liz.

'Romancing,' said Peter.

'With Merlin making spells,' went on Liz.

'You don't believe in him being a magician,' scoffed Peter.

'Why not,' said Dalip, 'it's over a thousand years ago. Why shouldn't they have had secrets then we know nothing about?'

'Rubbish,' said Peter.

'Stop arguing and enjoy the view,' said Gillian. 'Isn't it lovely?'

'Apart from the litter,' said Peter.

'Wouldn't you think people would have more respect!' exclaimed Dalip. 'Look at that large piece of yellow paper blowing about.'

'I'll pick it up,' said Liz.

'Why are people so mucky?' added Dalip.

'I say, there's funny writing on this,' said Liz.

'Let's look,' said Dalip, 'Coo, yes.'

'That's not ordinary paper, that's parchment,' said Gillian.

'From King Arthur's fish and chips,' said Peter.

'You could be right,' said Dalip. 'It could be from King Arthur's time, that's Latin on there.'

'What's the other writing?' asked Liz.

'I don't know,' said Dalip.

'It's very like Welsh,' remarked Gillian. 'I learned it as a child in Wales.'

'Let's take it and show Old Jilks at school. He'll know,' suggested Dalip.

'No,' said Gillian, 'this could be an important discovery. Let's keep it to ourselves for a bit and see what we can find out. It might make us famous.'

'Famous idiots,' said Peter.

'You never know,' said Dalip, 'I agree with Gill.'

'So do I,' said Liz.

'Let me work on it,' said Gillian.

Gillian met the gang a week after they had arrived home. 'I'm getting on fine,' she said. 'With the help of a Latin dictionary and a Welsh one. I think I know what it is already.'

'What?' they asked excitedly.

'It's a recipe for a drink,' she told them.

'King Arthur's beer,' suggested Peter.

'No, it's called Merlin's Brew,' said Gillian.

'Great!' said Liz.

Another week later she said, 'I think I've solved it. It's a mixture of spices, herbs and wild plants. I think I've got them right.'

'Can we make the brew?' asked Dalip.

'Why not,' said Gillian, 'if we can find everything.'

'You'll poison us,' said Peter.

The gang searched health food shops and the countryside for the ingredients. The wild plants were the hardest. They were not sure whether they were the right ones. With the help of books from the library they hoped they were right. They did not want to seek the help of grown-ups to verify their discoveries. They just made sure with the books that none of the wild plants was poisonous, though Peter kept casting doubts about this. Finally, Gillian made the brew with well-water she found in a nearby village. They did not think modern tap water would be right.

'That's it,' she said.

'It looks ghastly,' remarked Peter. 'Like mud and vinegar.'

'Who's going to drink it?' asked Dalip.

'I will,' said Gillian, 'as I made it. It's a bad cook that can't lick her own fingers.'

'Okay,' said Dalip, 'I'll join you.'

'I'll see what happens to you,' said Peter.

'So will I,' said Liz.

'We can't drink it right away, of course,' said Gillian. 'We have to wait for a full moon.'

'What rubbish!' said Peter.

'We'll do it properly,' said Gillian.

On the next full moon, Gillian and Dalip drank the brew. It tasted horrible. But to Peter's surprise they did not drop down dead or become drunk or anything. 'What a waste of time,' he said.

The next day, in the Maths lesson the master put a long problem on the board. 'I have some books to mark,' he said. 'This will keep you busy for half an hour.'

Gillian looked at the board. 'The answer's seventeen point five one three two,' she said immediately.

'What?' said the master.

'The answer's seventeen point five one three two,' she repeated.

'It is, but how did you know, Gillian?'

'I just know.'

'Have you got the answer book?'

'No.'

Some of the class giggled.

'I'll put another problem up,' said the master.

As he finished writing on the board, Gillian said: 'The answer's one point two seven squared.'

'You must have the answer book,' he said.

'Search me,' said Gillian.

He did. 'I don't understand it,' he said. 'Normally I have to give you help with the simplest of problems. I'll put up the homework on the board.' He did.

Gillian looked at it and quickly circulated the working and answers round the form. The class grinned and sniggered in glee.

At break, she met Dalip in the playground. She told him about what had happened. 'That's odd,' he said, 'because I got full marks in a French dictation.'

Later that day, Dalip scored six goals in a football match while Gillian baked a better cake than the Home Economics mistress.

The following week the exams started. Gillian and Dalip got one hundred per cent in all their exams. The gang met.

'It must be Merlin's brew,' said Dalip.

'Bags, I try it,' said Peter.

'You'll have to wait for the full moon,' Gillian reminded him.

'Can't I try some anyhow?' urged Peter.

'No,' said Gillian. 'You must do it properly.'

Dalip and Gillian excelled in everything they did. The Headmaster called them in following their exam results and asked for an explanation. He said he had never known anything like it in twenty years of teaching and would they please stop doing the homework for the rest of their classes. They told him they were only working harder and he could get nothing further out of them. Then at the next full moon Peter and Elizabeth drank the brew and also had super brainpower. 'No wonder King Arthur was so famous,' said Dalip, 'it was Merlin's brew.'

By now the Press had got on to their powers. 'Superkids' ran a headline in the local paper and it was soon picked up by the national papers.

'We shall have to tell,' said Gillian.

'No,' said Peter, 'it's such fun. Let's not tell anyone yet.'

'I think we should use it to solve world problems,' said Dalip 'Just think, we might help the world to peace. I have had a plan in the back of my mind all day which I think I will send to the Prime Minister.'

'If we could,' said Gillian. 'I have been thinking of how to solve the pollution problems.'

But the next day they were called to the Head's office. Some important-looking men sat with him. 'You must tell us what is happening,' said one of them.

'Not yet,' said Dalip. 'We think we can help the world.'

'Why not help your country first?' the Headmaster asked.

'No,' said Gillian, 'we must help all mankind.'

'Then I must warn you that you are being watched by a foreign power and we will have to watch you ourselves in case they try to kidnap you. I think I had better see your parents.'

Dalip looked at Gillian and then Peter and Liz. He could see the resigned look in their faces. 'All right,' he said, 'come home with us and we'll tell you.'

Gillian's mother met her at the door. 'Has school finished?' she asked. 'You're home early! A good thing too, you can help me to tidy up your room. What a mess in there! What have you been doing? I've burnt some of the rubbish you've collected.'

'No,' said Gillian. She rushed upstairs, followed by Dalip. It's gone!' she yelled. 'Mum, what have you done with a yellow piece of paper?'

'I burnt all that rubbishy paper,' said her mother.

'Oh no!' said Dalip.

The men followed them in. 'We had a secret recipe,' said Gillian. 'It was called Merlin's Brew. It gave us the super brain. But my mother's burnt it.'

'With your super brain you can remember it,' said one of them.

'Yes,' exclaimed Dalip.

'I'll try,' said Gillian.

However, it was getting towards the end of the lunar month. Her powers were wearing thin. Try as she might, she could not remember the quantities – only the ingredients.

The Ministry men took away the list of ingredients and the Government scientists worked on the brew but could not make the magic potion.

Dalip, Gillian, Peter and Liz returned to being normal children.

'Just think what we might have done,' said John.

'I don't know,' said Peter, 'it got boring after a bit and I was beginning to be called a creep.'

'It might have been used for evil if we had been kidnapped,' said Gillian. 'I think the spirit of Merlin caused my mother to tidy my room.'

'Perhaps,' said Dalip.

The Loner

I have not always been a loner. Times were when people flocked round me for my company. Let me tell you how it happened.

One morning the alarm clock went off. So did the bedside table, the chair and the chest of drawers – followed by the wardrobe. Soon the bedroom was empty of furniture.

Luckily, the bed stayed so I fell asleep again. This was odd because I was already lying down.

At eight o'clock, I was woken by birds singing. They sang 'God Save the Queen' so I had to stand up. I thought I might as well get up. I opened my eyes. They looked funny inside! I yawned and stretched my arms – two metres one side and one and a half metres the other – until they reached the wall.

I put my feet on the floor. Then I put my legs; then my knees; then my arms. It looked odd with the rest of my body on the bed.

I jumped up and down until my breath came in short pants! I put the pants on. I can't stand long pants! Then I put on my T-shirt as it was warmer than my coffee-shirt.

I went downstairs to the bathroom. One second later, I was back upstairs again. My braces had caught in the top banister!

I cleaned my teeth. Then I put them in. They were my mother's! She had taken mine again. I always did think there was something false about her.

I washed my hair. It was all right until I put it in the spin dryer. It gave me quite a turn!

The post came. The postman could not get it through the letter-box; there was too much fence attached to it. Some were bills. I do not know why they keep sending them to my house: Bill does not live here any more.

The milkman put two pints on the step: one of lager and lime; the other of bitter.

I made myself a cup of tea. It was difficult sticking all those

55

little brown leaves together. The handle was the hardest. It kept breaking.

The newspaper came through the door. I swept up the mess. I keep telling the boy to put it through the letter-box, but he will not listen. The news was frightening. The Government had created one million jobs for school leavers; there was an extra five pence on a packet of fags; and the brewery had caught fire. I don't know why I read the paper, it always gives me a turn.

My Mum had left me no breakfast so I peeled a banana. Then I had another turn. Yes, I slipped on the peel and fell on the music centre. It was a long-play record so it made me late for school.

I missed assembly – not much, but I missed it. I entered the classroom. I put it in for the 100 metres and the long jump. There were four rows of tables; to say nothing of two rows of carrots and three of cabbages. On each table was a sheet of paper, together with a pillow of paper and a blanket of paper. There was also a pen. In mine were six sheep.

The teacher, Mr Boring, came in the door. He looked odd because the rest of us came in T-shirts and jeans. He cast his eyes round the room. Then he cast his nose and then his ears. 'Today,' he said, 'I'm going to give you a test.'

We took the smiles off our faces and laid them on the tables. His tests were stiff: they were on cardboard.

'Fill in this form, Jenkins,' he said.

'I've no spade, sir,' I replied.

'First of all, Geography. Where are the West Indies?'

'Why? Have you lost them, sir?' I asked.

'Fool!' he yelled. 'How do you get to the Bermuda Triangle?'

'By tube from Leicester Square. Then on the Inner Circle.'

'Fool!' He kicked me out.

The centre half threw me in again.

'History,' he said. 'Who was Florence Nightingale?'

'Just some bird,' I ventured.

'Why was Scott so long in getting back from the South Pole?'

'The 93 bus was late again.'

'Idiot! Now poetry. Add the next line: 'Her teeth were like the stars . . . .'

'They came out at night,' I suggested.

'Leave the room!' he shouted.

'I had no intention of taking it with me,' I said.

He took me to the Headmaster. He had three heads; the rest of the masters had one.

'This boy is an idiot!' Mr Boring told him.

'It's all due to practice,' I said.

The Headmaster looked over the top of his glasses. He could just see me through the froth. 'I see you've done badly in the tests, Jenkins,' he said.

'It's not my fault, sir. I can't remember anything.'

'Oh, and how long have you had this problem?'

'What problem?' I asked.

'Any more of this and I'll suspend you,' he threatened.

'They don't hang people any more,' I said.

Then he shook me by the hand, by the foot, and by the knee. We fell in a heap on the floor. 'Jenkins,' he said, 'it is time you entered the world of work.'

My face turned green; my knees went yellow; and my feet went red. I looked like an upside-down traffic light.

'I am too young to die,' I said.

'Don't worry, I'll give you a good report,' he said, and he let off a gun by my ear.

I shot out of the door.

I went home. A typical family scene met my eyes. 'Hello!' said the family scene.

'Hello,' said my left pupil.

There was Granny concreting the path. My mother was rewiring the bedroom. And my father was doing his knitting.

'I've left the school,' I told them.

'Where have you left it?' asked my father. 'I hope not in the front garden, Granny's doing the concreting.'

'I'm going to get a job.'

My father fainted.

'You'll make history in this family,' said my mother. 'None of the Jenkins has ever worked.'

'I'll teach him to shoplift,' said my father coming to.

'The doctor said he was to do nothing heavy,' said my mother.

I went out and caught a bus. It was surprisingly heavy.

The bus was packed. All ready to go on its holidays. It was worse when the conductor came up the stairs, followed by his orchestra. You couldn't sit down for trombones.

'Where to, mate?' he asked.

'The Job Centre,' I told him.

'What for?'

'I'm going to get a job.'

'Have they got jobs!' he yelled. He rushed off the bus. So did the driver and the rest of the passengers. I had to walk there.

When I got there I had to line up behind the orchestra. It took me two hours to get to the counter. 'One, two, three, four,' it went as I got up to it.

'I want a job,' I told the girl.

'You've come a bit late,' she said, 'this lot have taken all the best jobs. Unless you can drive a bus?'

'I'm a school leaver,' I said.

Her eyes lit up. She had a torch in her head. 'I've just the job!' she cried. 'They need a school leaver at the pig farm.'

'But what about the smell?'

'They'll soon get used to you.'

'Is it dirty work?'

'No, it's quite honest,' she said. 'I think this job will save your bacon.' She collapsed on the floor. 'I ham sure you will get it.' She rolled on the floor. 'I don't want to hog the job to myself.' She was in stitches. 'After all, you've got the right manure for the job,' she said, unpicking them. 'Now just trotter long.'

I left her laughing her head off; it looked funny rolling about on the floor. I walked to the pig farm.

A bloke in a cloth cap, chewing a piece of straw, met me. A dog was at his heels; a chicken was perched on his head; and a pig was on his shoulder. He looked me over. 'You need boots,' he said.

'The chemists?' I said. 'What for? Perfume?'

''Tis mucking out time,' he said. 'Can you do it?'

'I'm used to mucking about at school,' I told him.

'Good,' he said. He took me to a large shed. It was full of grunts and squeals. It was also full of something else: right up to the ankles. He gave me a shovel.

Four hours later, I had piled it up in a truck. It was back-breaking work. I broke at least three of my backs. I leant on my shovel for a rest. Then something else broke – the shaft of the shovel. I was standing on the top of the truck at the time. I fell right in it.

I soon had the bus home to myself. People came on, but suddenly got off before their stop. Finally, the conductor and the driver left and I had to walk home.

I had not been in the house five minutes before my mother and father were packing. They had to go to South America, they told me. Then Gran suddenly remembered she had to visit a relative.

Five months later they have not returned. Sometimes I go out for a walk but my friends suddenly need something on the other side of the street. As I have said, I have not always been a loner. It started like this: one morning the alarm clock went off. So did the bedside table, the chair . . . .

The Bell

The light was fading and a gusty wind blew a fine drizzle into
their faces, but they would not go home. If they went to Ian's they
could not escape his brothers – loud, boisterous and full of
demands to play games, usually games involving some sort of
fighting, which Jayne hated. But Jayne's was even worse; there
was Granny Aggie, Aggie the Naggy. Aggie was small, silver-
haired, always dressed in black and always sitting in her
armchair, knitting and watching. Aggie watched everybody for
signs of any wrongdoing, such as eating between meals, not
sitting straight in a chair, speaking too loudly or wanting to
watch sport on television. But most of all Aggie watched Ian and
Jayne. If their hands touched, Aggie would cough a loud warning;
if they attempted to sit it out until Jayne's parents were ready for
bed and Aggie ready to snore through the epilogue, she would
start her gentle hints.

'Time you were off home, young man. You'll be fit for nothing
in the morning. I was in bed at nine o'clock sharp at your age.'

So Ian and Jayne stayed out in the gloom and rain, but the
wind blew harder and the rain began to soak their clothes.

'Let's go in the church,' said Jayne. Ian was doubtful; he
had never been to church in his life. 'Come on, at least it's dry
there.'

Jayne pulled him towards the huge, metal-studded door. She
turned the handle and pushed. The door opened slowly, creaking
like a horror movie sound effect. They looked round nervously;
they could just see the rows of pews, but the font shone white in
the last of the daylight that penetrated the grimy stained-glass
windows.

'It's scary in here,' said Ian.

'Only people are scary and there aren't any in here,' said
Jayne.

She was wrong. As their eyes focused, they saw an old lady, her white head bent in prayer. She was in a pew only ten metres away.

'It's Ag the Nag,' said Ian, and started for the door.

'No chance,' said Jayne. 'Ag's at home in bed downstairs. She's had one of her do's again.'

'What's she doing?' whispered Ian, pointing to the old lady.

'Praying for something,' said Jayne. 'She's asking God to make her good.'

'I shouldn't think there's much chance of her not being good at her age,' said Ian.

'Not that sort of good, you fool.'

'Let's get out of here,' said Ian.

Just then there were voices at the church door. Their escape was cut off.

'In here,' said Jayne, and she led the way to the vestry. Now there was a heavy curtain to hide behind, they both felt more easy. But not for long. Through a hole in the curtains they could see that two men had entered the church; they were making their way to the vestry. One of them Jayne recognised as the vicar, the Reverend Simmons.

'They'll think we've come to nick their candlesticks,' said Ian.

'Up here,' said Jayne, and she led the way up the tiny, dark, spiral staircase that began in the corner of the vestry.

They climbed and climbed in silence; eventually, the darkness lifted into gloom. Their way was stopped by a wooden platform. There was a small trapdoor in the platform. They opened it, squeezed into the bell tower and lay on the boards, exhausted by their climb.

About a metre above their heads was a huge bell; they could see others a little further away.

'What if they went off?' said Ian, staring at the clapper that was almost as big as his head.

'You mean ring. Don't worry. They only ring them on Sundays and Tuesday nights when they practise.'

Jayne stood up, making sure not to bash her head on the nearest bell. She put her hands on its smooth shape; it was cold. She gave it a slight push. It stirred uneasily; the vibrations ran up her arms.

'Come and feel this bell; it's smooth and freezing; how did they make it?'

'I'd rather feel you; at least you're warm,' said Ian.

'Not in church, you don't.'

'This isn't church,' said Ian. 'We could hide here.'

'You mean set up home?'

'Yeh. We could bring the camping stove and a torch. I bet nobody ever comes up here.'

'We wouldn't have far to go home after we were married, I suppose,' said Jayne.

'No, I'm serious,' said Ian. 'It's definitely the most secret place in the village.'

'Sounds like playing mummies and daddies,' said Jayne doubtfully.

'It's definitely better than facing Ag or my brothers.'

'Okay, you win. Your turn to put out the cat and milk bottles. I'm off to bed.'

For the next four months the belfry was a refuge from rain, cold, Ag and the roaring boys. Soon it contained a camping stove, two small canvas chairs and two torches. It took about half an hour to make a cup of coffee, but it tasted all the better for the wait.

As the days grew longer, they were able to slip into the church in daylight. Then they could see the countryside through the slit in the bell tower. They were frighteningly high. The whole valley grew greener and more beautiful as the weeks past.

'I'd like a view like this when I'm married,' said Jayne.

'We'll live at the top of a tower block,' said Ian.

'You're not very romantic, are you?'

'I am if I'm given the chance.'

'You don't even know what it means. Let's go, you fool; you'll start the bell off.'

It was the day after the Whitsun holiday. Jayne and Ian made their way to the belfry in silence. Jayne had been crying; her face was white, and a mascara stain made her look as if she had been in a fight.

'Just forget about her. Maybe she'll soon be dead,' said Ian.

'I wouldn't wish that on her, and she really is ill. Mum's been up with her most of the past three nights. I don't know how she stands it.'

'Being ill's not stopped her nagging,' said Ian bitterly.

'You don't know the half of it; she wasn't moaning nearly as much when you came.'

They climbed the belfry steps, taking care not to be seen, and determined to forget Ag the Nag for an hour or two. They made a cup of coffee, and sat drinking and staring out at the fields.

'You can see nearly to Manchester,' said Jayne. 'I wouldn't mind staying here for a month.'

They relapsed into silence. Jayne lay face down on the boards, looking through the sides of the holes where the ropes stretched down into the vestry six metres below. Ian sat beside her, holding her hand and stroking her hair. Soon she fell asleep, and he sat watching her breathing deeply. Eventually he felt drowsy himself; it was a hot day, and the belfry was small and stuffy.

When the bell boomed into life, Jayne at first thought it was a nightmare. Immediately, both she and Ian were awake and being shaken and deafened; the whole belfry seemed to be moving – the noise was hideous.

'Keep flat,' shouted Ian, between the tremendous booms.

They lay on their backs, their fingers in their ears. They watched the great bell move up to almost right angles, before it came swinging down and sending a boom of sound and vibration through their bodies.

'The place is falling apart,' Jayne whimpered. Ian did not hear her, but saw her frightened face. He was terrified too; it would be a ridiculous death, to be plunged to the stone floor of the vestry.

Ian motioned Jayne to turn over, so she would not see the bell. She peered through a knothole and could see the vicar. He pulled the rope slowly and methodically, sending shock-waves of noise through their bodies. Then he paused for about twenty seconds, before repeating the torture. Jayne wanted to scream out to him to stop, but now she was almost paralysed by the shock-waves.

At last the vicar stopped and walked slowly away. They lay in stunned silence; the belfry still seemed to be on the move. It was five full minutes before Ian said: 'Well, it's stopped, and we're alive.'

'Only just,' said Jayne. 'I feel as if my head's been the clapper.'

'I thought you said they only practised on Tuesday nights,' said Ian.

'That wasn't practising; there was only the vicar, and he only rang the big one about every half minute.'

'What did he want to do that for?'

'Maybe it's instead of jogging, to give him a bit of exercise. What time is it?'

'About six. We've been here four hours. You had a really good sleep. It will set you up for the night if you get disturbed by Ag.'

Ian took Jayne home. Her mother opened the door while they were still walking up the drive.

'Where've you been? We've been looking all over for you.'

'We've been walking,' said Ian quickly.

'What's up?' said Jayne.

'Your gran's dead, that's what's up,' said her mum.

'Oh, no!' said Jayne.

'I'm sorry,' muttered Ian, looking at the tarmac.

'Well, it can't be helped,' said Jayne's mum; she began to cry and Jayne went to put her arm round her.

'No, don't do that; it'll make me worse. I'll get over it. She was a good woman. She'd had a long life. She died peaceful in the end.'

'When did she die, Mum?'

'I found her dead in the chair. Her mouth was open. I hope she hadn't been trying to shout for help.'

'I shouldn't think so. I suppose most people die with their mouths open.'

'What do you know about it? And you gallivanting round while she was dying. It beats me you didn't hear the passing bell.'

'The what bell?' said Jayne.

'The passing bell to show there was a death. It was always your gran's wish that the vicar rang the passing bell when she went – just like in the old days,' she said. Jayne's mum's voice sank to a whisper as the tears came again. 'I wanted you to go and tell the vicar. Instead I had to leave her and go myself. What your dad'll say I don't know.' She turned on her heels and went inside. Jayne hesitated.

'I'd better go in, I suppose.'

'Okay,' said Ian. 'She nearly did for us in the end, then.'

'Yes, it's just as if she wanted a last go at us.'

'It was a pretty good go. My ears are still ringing.'

'We'll go and get our stuff out tomorrow. I wouldn't dare stay in there again.'

'In any case,' said Ian, 'when things have settled down, I can come here now Ag . . . . I mean your gran . . . . won't be spying on us.'

'Maybe she's spying on us from somewhere else.'

'As long as we can't see or hear her I don't mind much.'

'Maybe not. But if we ever get married in a church it'll remind me of her, especially when the bells ring.'

'Yes, it will. In a way she's going to be with us for ever.'

The Wedding

'Oh, Mum, it's all green!' Anne-Marie rushed in.

'What's green?' asked her mother.

'My hair! Look, it's supposed to be blonde.'

'That's Antoine.'

'I asked him specially for blonde for the wedding.'

'It's his English, dear. You know how he shaved me down to the crown. Like a lawn mower over the head. I only asked for a trim.'

'I can't be married looking like this!'

'You often look like that.'

'I don't want a punk wedding.'

'Well, Ted will be in his leathers.'

'I know. That's his choice – to be in leathers. His masculine look, he calls it. But I wanted to look traditional. It's my special day.' She began to cry.

'Cheer up. Here's something blue.'

'They're Gran's old bloomers!'

'That's right. I married your father in them.'

'I can't wear them.'

'Nobody'll see them under your dress.'

'Oh, Mum.'

'Now calm down. You'll ruin your make-up.'

Downstairs, Mr Tompkins was sampling the champagne he was supposed to have taken to the reception hall. 'Just to make sure it isn't rubbish,' he told Nigel. 'You can be sold rubbish these days.'

'There's a wine lake in Europe,' said Nigel.

'I'd like to go there,' said Mr Tompkins.

'I'm going to video the whole wedding, Dad.'

'Good, son. Try a drop of this.' Mr Tompkins fell heavily into a chair. He shot out quickly again clutching his behind. 'Cor! I've been stung or something.'

'You've sat on Gran's hat,' said Nigel. He removed a ten-centimetre hatpin from Mr Tompkins' rear.

'What does she want to use those things for?'

'Look what you've done to her hat!'

The floral hat was as flat as a table mat. Framed, it would have made a good collage.

'Can it be mended?' slurred Mr Tompkins.

'I'll try, Dad. I'll use some lolly sticks and that double-sided sticky tape they use on "Blue Peter".' He whisked the hat off, eager for some new challenge to his ingenuity, forgetting the video camera for a moment.

Gran bustled in. 'Have you seen my hat? I've lost my hat.'

'No,' lied Mr Tompkins.

'I bet it's our Nigel. Up to his tricks again.' She dashed out.

Anne-Marie came downstairs. She had concealed most of the green hair, apart from a few wisps at the nape, under her veil.

'Doesn't she look lovely?' sighed Mrs Tompkins.

'There's a bit hanging out at the back,' observed Mr Tompkins.

'Where?' Anne-Marie clutched at her rear, fearing the bloomers.

'That's her train. It took me ages to get that right,' said Mrs Tompkins.

'This is the age of the train,' laughed Mr Tompkins, collapsing into the chair again.

Nigel came in and slipped Gran's hat on to the sideboard. He had replaced a few of the flowers with some from Anne-Marie's bouquet.

'Are the cars here yet?' asked Mrs Tompkins.

'Never mind the cars, where's my hat?' asked Gran, coming into the room.

'It's here, Gran. On the sideboard,' said Mrs Tompkins.

'It wasn't before. Have you been up to something, Nigel?'

'No, Gran.'

Gran jammed the hat on her head. She went to the mirror and stuck a hatpin in like a bayonet. She did not need a hatpin – the double-sided tape was holding the hat firmly to her hair.

'Are the cars here?' asked Mrs Tompkins again.

'There's a van outside,' said Nigel.

There was a knock at the door. Nigel went to open it. The man who stood outside asked: 'Where's the blushing bride then?'

'It's the cars!' shouted Mrs Tompkins. She rushed outside and saw the van. 'Where's the Rolls?' she asked.

'Ah, we had a bit of trouble with the ignition,' said the man. 'Even the jump leads wouldn't get it going this morning.' He waved vaguely at the van. It had 'Jackson's Removals' on the side. 'We brought this!'

'I'm not going in a van!' shouted Anne-Marie.

'There's a nice settee in the back,' said the man. 'Real leather.'

Anne-Marie sat on the front doorstep. 'No! No! No!' she yelled.

Ted roared by on his motor bike with the best man on the pillion. He waved. 'There's Ted,' said Mrs Tompkins.

Anne-Marie shot up. 'He's not supposed to see me till I come down the aisle,' she sobbed.

'What are we waiting for?' asked Gran.

'I want a shot of you all leaving the house,' said Nigel.

'Can't Dad drive me in our car?' wailed Anne-Marie.

'Your Dad's in no fit state to drive. Do wake up, Herbert,' she said, shaking him. 'Come on, dear, Ted'll be waiting,' she said to her daughter.

'No,' said Anne-Marie.

'This van's been all the way to Venice,' said the man. 'I've got the sticker.'

'There you are, see, it's special,' said Mrs Tompkins.

Mr Tompkins staggered to the door.

'There's no Rolls,' said Mrs Tompkins.

'I must have bread with my soup,' said Mr Tompkins.

'No, the car. We're going in a van.'

'It'll be cheaper,' said the man. 'I thought you could all get in the one.'

'I'm supposed to arrive last with Dad,' said Anne-Marie.

'Well, if you get in first you can get out last,' stated the man. 'There's a choice of the ramp or the hydraulic lift. Can you hurry? The tachometer's ticking over.'

'Come on,' said Mr Tompkins. He pulled Anne-Marie after him.

Nigel shot out of the van first to film the party going under the lych-gate. 'Just walk naturally,' he urged.

A strong wind blew Anne-Marie's train on to a holly bush.

'Walk forward,' said Nigel.

Anne-Marie did. There was a ripping sound. Ten square centimetres of Gran's blue bloomers were revealed. Nobody bothered to tell Anne-Marie – so as not to spoil the occasion. She could be difficult at times.

Anne-Marie stood at the church door. Her father leaned up against the doorpost, using the wedding ceremony programme he had been given as a fan. The organist was pummelling away on the 'Voluntary', oblivious to the vicar's signals that the ceremony could begin. In the end the vicar had to stomp up into the organ loft to get things going.

As Anne-Marie stepped into the aisle, she caught sight of Ted. He was in his helmet. This thought was not far from her mind as she slowly progressed towards the vicar.

'Take your helmet off in church,' she hissed as they stood together.

Ted just smiled at her.

'Take your helmet off!' she whispered.

'He's got a boil on his nose,' said the best man. 'He doesn't want it to show up on the video.'

'Oh,' said Anne-Marie.

The short-sighted vicar, who had married many assorted couples lately, thought Ted's orange helmet was his hair and quickly whisked off into the ceremony. 'Dearly beloved, we are gathered together . . . '

Halfway through this, standing became too much for Mr Tompkins – he subsided into a pew. Mrs Tompkins was praying that he would not snore.

Proceedings were then held up by a violent bout of sneezing from Gran. The real flowers in her hat had brought on a hay fever attack. The vicar jerked intermittently towards the 'Edward, wilt though have this woman' part. Ted just grinned at him. He could not hear a word under his helmet. Thinking the groom must be a mute, the vicar proceeded, taking the smile as affirmation.

On 'Who giveth this woman . . . .' Mrs Tompkins prodded her husband. He woke up sharply and shouted: 'I do, mate.'

The vicar then read out the 'I, Edward, take thee, Anne-Marie . . . .' part for the mute Ted. Anne-Marie repeated her part and the best man produced the ring and promptly dropped it. Everyone joined in the search, except Mr Tompkins who had dropped off to sleep again. Anne-Marie's ten square centimetres of blue became twenty.

Outside, the next party was waiting to come in and some of them were peering round the door.

Finally, after twenty minutes, the ring was found under the lectern. The marriage service proceeded without another hitch, except that the organist played 'Here Comes the Bride' as Anne-Marie came out, causing panic among the waiting party who thought they should be inside. This caused a mêlée on the steps outside somewhat akin to a rugby union match highlight.

Eventually the right marriage party stood for Nigel's video – except for Mr Tompkins who sat in a flower-tub. Anne-Marie clasped Ted to her and kissed his perspex visor. They were man and wife.

Vicky Mills

Vicky Mills didn't seem to care a damn about anything. A couple
of teachers who could put up with her called her 'irrepressible'
and shrugged off her cheek, but most of them called her 'insolent'
and 'a disgrace to the school'.

Nobody said much against her while she was there, though.
Even the teachers who hated her were wary of her, and
complained about her mostly when she was not in lessons.
I think if you really don't care then you have an advantage over
people – they are scared of what you might say back if they
criticise you.

There was plenty of chance to have a go at Vicky when she was
not there, though, because she had about two days off every week
and spent a fair amount of the rest of the time being sent home.

For instance, the first day of last term she turned up dressed
very carefully. She must have taken some care to manage to
break almost every school rule in one go. She was wearing bright
red lipstick, loads of face make-up and enough blue eyeshadow to
have painted a whole row of chorus girls. She also had green
trousers and a ring on each finger – the sort of rings you win for
second prize in the hoop-la at the fair.

Somehow she survived assembly – I think most of the teachers
did not want to be the first to 'notice' her, because they were sure
to come in for a mouthful of abuse.

When we were waiting for Mr Soames to come and try to teach
us History, Vicky came and sat herself next to me. I wasn't very
keen, but I daren't say much, because she was obviously in one of
her aggressive moods.

'You'll not last till break looking like that,' I said.

'Looking like what, George?'

'Well . . . . you know . . . . all that make-up and your trousers
and things.'

'Don't you like it, George? Don't you love me any more?'

'It's all right,' I said, regretting mentioning it, 'but old Soames won't be too pleased.'

'Oh, well, I don't fancy him, so it don't matter. I'm pleased you like it though, George.'

She was embarrassing. She twisted everything you said; actually, she wasn't bad-looking; if she didn't bury herself in make-up and act as aggressive as a prizefighter she would have been all right.

Soames was only ten minutes into revising the 'Iron Age Man' when he suddenly stopped and stared at Vicky. 'You, girl,' he said, breathing heavily and with his eyes glinting behind his huge glasses. 'Are you a pupil at this school or are you not?'

'Have you forgotten me in the holidays, sir? It's me, Vicky, your favourite pupil. Oh sir, you must remember me.'

'Go and present yourself to Miss Jenkins immediately, and see what she thinks of your . . . . whatever you've got on your face and legs.' Soames knew that his main job was to get Vicky out of the room quickly. He would not get much change out of her by arguing; if he started to be sarcastic, old Vicky would match him any day.

'Righto, sir,' said Vicky unexpectedly. 'I'll go and tell her you're interested in me legs.'

Mr Soames didn't reply; he stood there stiff and fierce-faced; perhaps he thought that if he moved steam might start coming out of his ears.

Vicky took about five minutes to go. First, she knocked over her chair and carefully and slowly picked it up. When she was near the door, she suddenly came back and started peering under her desk.

'What's the matter, girl?' said Soames in a strangled sort of voice.

'I've lost Wilson, sir. You stolen Wilson, George?' Wilson was her little toy tiger; she had deliberately left it on her seat. 'Got him, sir,' she shouted. 'Wilson wards off evil spirits, sir. Do you want to see him?'

She held out the miniature tiger to Mr Soames.

'Get out!' screamed Soames, losing control of himself.

'I'm going, I'm going . . . . you must have got out of bed the wrong side, sir.'

Of course she left the door open and as Soames went to shut it she poked her head back into the room, said 'Sorry, sir,' and then slammed it shut in his face.

After she had gone, there was a couple of minutes' silence while Soames fought to plug the volcano that had got going inside him. Then he gave us a lecture about Vicky. It was the usual teacher lecture about Vicky. She was mad, couldn't help it, and we weren't to take any notice of her.

It wasn't Vicky herself that the teachers were scared of, although she certainly upset them enough – but the effect that she might have on the rest of us. They thought that we all might start behaving like Vicky. So they kept on about how mad she was, how she wouldn't get a job, and how she was going to get expelled.

Actually, I don't think they dared to expel her, because they had tried suspending her for a fortnight and she came more often in the fortnight of her suspension than she had ever been before. Ours is quite a big school, over fifteen hundred kids, and Vicky easily got herself lost in it. As she was suspended she was not expected in lessons, so they didn't even know where she should be, let alone where she was. She hung around chatting at breaks and dinner times and during lessons she would be around the PE or Art area – anywhere there was likely to be kids to chat to. Every time she was spotted by a teacher she would be told to clear off, and she did – to a different area of the school. In the end they had one teacher almost full-time on Vicky-spotting; I think the teachers were pretty relieved when her suspension was finished and she could go back to coming only part-time.

No sooner had Soames finished his lecture about Vicky, when she came bouncing back into the room.

'Can't find Miss Jenkins, sir. I've searched high and low.'

She smelt of fags even from where I was sitting. I am sure she had spent the last quarter of an hour in the toilet smoking.

'I'll find her myself,' shouted Soames, and strode out of the door, furious.

'D'ya want a fag, George?' she asked, as she sat on the desk and started swinging her green legs.

'Don't be daft, Vicky.'

'What's up with you? You scared?'

She was at her worst when she started to show off like that. None of us took as much notice of her as she thought we should, considering how she behaved, so if she had done something such as annoy Soames she often started to show off.

Anyway, she managed to last till dinner time before they finally got her off the premises. She came back about half an hour before the end of afternoon school; she had re-arranged her face a bit but had not washed much of the make-up off. She had swopped her trousers for a very old school skirt with tears in it; she had probably spent some of her dinner time making the tears.

And they let her stay! All she was told was: 'That's better but there's still room for improvement.' Actually it wasn't better at all, but she had worn them down, as she usually did.

Vicky lived about a mile outside of the town – in a barn. Well, I suppose it wasn't a barn really but it was big, dilapidated, and surrounded by all sorts of clutter – old farm machinery, old bikes and usually a few mangy horses: sometimes tied up to the pieces of machinery; sometimes running loose in the scrubby patch of grass between the house and the road. There was often a couple of little kids clambering about the machinery who must have been Vicky's brother and sister. I had never seen any sign of a dad or a mum.

That was until I was going home one day when I got a puncture – just outside the path to Vicky's house. Well, I cursed and kicked a bit and then started to push the bike three miles home. I had not gone ten metres before I heard somebody shout: 'George, hang on a minute. What's up?' When she shouted I knew it was Vicky before I turned round; she had a voice like a dalek with stomach ache. After ten minutes arguing, she persuaded me to push my bike down to her house where, she told me, she could find a spare inner tube, or even a wheel if it was necessary.

'We'll have a drink first,' she said, when I had parked my bike against the big tree about ten metres from her house. The roots of the tree were sticking out in places and the two little kids were jumping from one root to another, trying to avoid putting their feet on the ground.

'Look at them two,' said Vicky. 'I'll have to swill 'em down before I get their tea.'

'Ain't your mum in then?'

Vicky laughed, or rather made a forced cackling sound.

'Depends what you mean by "in". She's in the house all right, but she's not "in" in the head. She's wappy, didn't you know?'

I had guessed old Vicky had a few problems at home, otherwise she would not have been so keen to come to school when she was suspended.

'Hey, our Vicky,' said one of the kids playing on the tree root, 'dad's left some fish for our tea, but our mam's buried it in the back garden.' The kid didn't seem all that put out by his tea being buried; he said it in the way you would tell somebody the time. Vicky wasn't too pleased, though.

'Oh Lord!' she said. 'I thought we'd cured her of that.'

She shoved the front door open – it seemed to be half-off its hinges – and I followed her reluctantly inside. It was pretty dark in Vicky's house – and very full. It was dark because the windows were small and dirty; it was full of furniture, most of it junk. It looked like a second-hand auction room – settees, chairs, grandfather clocks, not set out in any pattern, but just shoved into any available space.

'What you done with that fish, you wappy old woman?' said Vicky.

At first I thought she was talking to me, but then I noticed behind a grandfather clock, a ragbag of a woman was moving to and fro in an old black rocking-chair. She stopped rocking for a moment when Vicky shouted, and pulled the rusty-looking shawl round her shoulders a bit tighter. Then she started rocking again and making a low moaning sort of noise; it sounded like a deaf person trying to hum a tune.

'No use talking to her,' said Vicky. 'She's right off her head, a real creamer, a complete and utter nutter, mad as . . . .'

'How long has she been like that?' I interrupted, embarrassed by Vicky's having a go at her mum while she was sitting only two metres away.

'Ages, only she's got worse in the last two years. We're trying to have her put away, but my dad ain't got time to get round to it. He's too busy.'

'Doing what?'

I was beginning to feel slightly more at ease. Vicky wasn't like she was at school. She seemed more certain, more in control. I got the impression she was the boss in this barn of a house, and she didn't need to show off.

Ten minutes later we were sitting under the tree drinking tea and eating chocolate biscuits. I had noticed they had cupboards full of biscuits and tins of food. Some of the stuff in the room was quite valuable as well. They were not poor; it was just that everything was a mess, nothing organised.

'What's your dad do?' I asked again; Vicky hadn't answered my question first time because she'd been busy giving the kids their tea – a packet of biscuits and a bottle of pop – she had obviously given up the idea of trying to find where the mad woman had buried the fish.

'Buys and sells stuff, that sort of thing.'

Vicky seemed a bit evasive, most unusual for her; but as it happened it wasn't long before I found out more about her dad's business.

I had swopped the busted inner tube for a good one, and was pumping up the tyre when Vicky came and knelt beside me.

'George, do us a favour. Say you bought a white pony off us a fortnight ago and that you've just come to look at another for your sister.'

'I haven't got a sister. What you on about? Who should I tell all this rubbish to?'

'These two that are coming down the drive. That's three times they've been. Do it, George, there's a good lad.'

Vicky was whispering but quite loudly; she sounded a bit desperate.

Well, I hadn't time to say any more before this car drew up under the tree. Out got a tall bloke with a big nose and a smart grey suit. After him came a girl about Vicky's age, but she looked about as different from Vicky as you could imagine. She was tall, wore a smart blue trouser-suit and carried a dinky umbrella. I was pretty sure I had never seen her at our school.

The girl and the bloke came up to Vicky and me. Vicky stood up, but I stayed bent down pumping the tyre, embarrassed and puzzled.

'I still don't see Bongo,' said this girl. She talked in a snotty, bored sort of voice. 'Where do you say he is this time?' She looked round at the clutter and the two horses tied to an old binder.

'Sold him,' said Vicky, hard-faced and defiant.

'Sold him where?' said the girl indignantly. 'You said you were going to use him for riding.'

'As a matter of fact,' said Vicky, 'I sold him to this gentleman here; he's so pleased with him that he's come looking for another like him. Isn't that right, mister?'

I don't go red very often, but I felt my face start to burn and my hands were sticky with sweat.

'Er, yes, that's right,' I mumbled. It was bad enough being called 'gentleman' and 'mister' by old Vicky; but to be claiming I'd bought a horse called Bongo (at least I assumed it was a horse) was even worse.

'Where do you live, young man?' asked the man suspiciously. During the next ten minutes I gave the most unconvincing performance you could possibly imagine. I first told them that Bongo lived in a stable with three other ponies, and a few minutes later claimed he had his own personal little paddock to roam in. He had also won third prize at the Bexley Gymkhana and ate a bag of oats for his supper every night. I felt as if I was being interviewed by the police; certainly any jury would have convicted me of lying. But there was no proof, despite the contradictions in my story, that I was not the proud owner of a white pony called Bongo. In the end the man and his daughter reluctantly climbed back into their car and drove off. I was weak at the knees. I sat down under the tree.

'Where is Bongo?' I asked. I didn't even sound mad; I was too exhausted.

'Either the Frogs have eaten him or he's in about a thousand tins of cat food,' said Vicky. 'If they come here again we'll have them shipped off as well. That bitch would make a good few tins of "Woof" or whatever they call it.'

Well, it took about half an hour, but I finally managed to understand Vicky's dad's business. He was a sort of horse dealer, buying horses and ponies wherever he could and then either flying them out to France (where apparently they ate them with the same relish as they ate snails) or selling them to some pet food organisation. At this moment, her dad had gone to Wales to bargain for a load of ponies to make the chunks of lean meat to go with the marrowbone jelly.

'I don't see what it matters to folks what you do with their horses if you've bought 'em.'

'Don't you, George? Well, I wish you'd tell 'em that. It's these folks that buy ponies for their kids and then can't afford to keep them; they're the biggest trouble. They advertise something like "loveable pony called Rastus going cheap to good home" and then my dad takes me along and he tells them he's looking for a pony for his daughter to ride. I have to say what a lovely little chap it is and then we buy it and in a week it's in the "Woof"-making machine. Some of 'em, like that silly cow who's just gone, keep coming back to see how it's getting on. That really gets on my nerves.'

I could see how it got on Vicky's nerves. She explained it all quietly, but a bit sadly as well. Then she got up and said she would have to sort the kids out and square round a bit. Just before I pushed my bike away, she said: 'Soon I'm going to get out of here; I'll be getting a flat in town. You can come and see me then, eh George?'

'Okay,' I said and grinned at her.

I knew I could say 'okay' without much worry; I knew as well as Vicky there was not a chance of her getting away from the barn, the kids, the mad mum and the pony-buying routine.

I liked old Vicky, I thought, as I rode home. But I liked her better outside school than in it. She wasn't so fierce, and didn't show off so much. I knew that by the end of the week she would do something at school that would embarrass me and make me want to screw her neck off.

Mr Mobbs and the Strange Power

A tremendous racket of scraping chairs, cat-calls and laughter came out of Mr Mobbs' classroom. In the corridor outside, the Headmaster paced up and down. Amid the noise he could hear Jenkins calling: 'Oi! Mobbo, I 'aven't done no 'omework as I've lost your stupid books.' The weak voice of Mr Mobbs followed. The Headmaster could not hear what he said because of the laughter.

The bell went and the class rushed out, knocking over chairs and bursting through the door like a steam train crashing through a crossing-gate. They slowed to the sedate pace of a rowing boat as they met the Headmaster and pretended to be quiet, orderly pupils keeping to the left of the corridor.

Mr Mobbs sat slumped at his desk. He was only one and a half metres tall – Jenkins was nearly two metres – and although only 28 was going prematurely grey. He was a Cambridge scholar of Latin and Greek but had been forced to teach Mathematics in order to find a job. This was only the second lesson of the day and he was utterly exhausted.

The Headmaster bustled in: 'Really, Mobbs,' he spluttered, 'you must discipline your classes. How can I bring visitors round the school? I will give you a week, then I must report the matter to the governors.'

Mr Mobbs had been trying for three years to discipline classes. As well as his lack of height he was shy with a light, high-pitched voice. He envied the tough men and women in the school who could bully pupils into submission, but he could be no more like them than fly. He was a very christian man; he tried to love his neighbour and he hated punishing pupils. He put his head on the cool of the table top. He could not master 4C or 4D. In a week he could be out of a job.

He did not bother to go to the staffroom for a coffee. As the bell went for the end of break he wearily went up the stairs to his

75

next classsoom, carrying 4D's scrawled-on exercise books. When
he had reached the top step there was a great cry and Jenkins
came round the corner, pursued by Morris. Jenkins had
'borrowed' Morris's bag and Morris was not pleased about it.
Mr Mobbs' small mouth opened, his voice piped a weak 'Jen
. . . .' Then all the wind was knocked out of him by Jenkins'
elbow; he crumpled and rolled down a complete flight of stairs.

He was in a coma for a week. No one from school visited him in
hospital during that time. Then he came round. The doctor said
that he had been badly concussed but no damage had been done
to the brain. After a further week's observation, he could
probably go back to school. In the peace and quiet of a private
room that was the best week he could remember for years.

At breakfast on the morning he was due to return to school he
felt he must give in his notice and not wait for the Headmaster to
sack him. But something strange immediately happened. His
landlady said: 'I'm sorry there's no milk for your cornflakes but
the milkman hasn't been yet.'

'There is milk in the fridge, Mrs Danby,' he was surprised to
find himself saying in a firm and deep voice. 'You are saving it for
your husband. As I am paying you a great deal from board and
lodging I think I should come first.' Mrs Danby looked at him in
amazement but she went and fetched the milk. He sat back
stunned.

Then on his way to school he called in at his local tobacconist's
for some of his favourite pipe tobacco. 'I'm sorry your brand has
gone up five pence,' the tobacconist said.

'Yes,' said Mr Mobbs, amazed at himself, 'but you bought this
packet in at the old price and as a valued customer I think . . . .'

'I didn't,' blustered the tobacconist.

'Don't lie,' said Mr Mobbs.

'Oh, very well then,' said the tobacconist. He flung the packet
down.

Mr Mobbs went out of the shop feeling three metres tall.

At school the Headmaster greeted him: 'How nice to see you fit
and well again, Mr Mobbs.'

'You are not thinking that,' said Mr Mobbs. 'You are thinking
what a pity he has come back. Why could he not have been
injured permanently so that I could get a new Maths teacher?'

'Really, Mr Mobbs,' spluttered the Head.

'Now I must get on with my teaching,' said Mr Mobbs
positively.

He strode out into the corridor. Then he stopped perplexed.
How could he have spoken to the Head like that? Then it came to

him: he had been able to see into the mind of Mrs Danby, the tobacconist and the Headmaster; he could tell what they were thinking.

In the staffroom Miss Oshodi greeted him: 'Oh, I'm so glad you're back.'

'You mean: What a pity that pathetic little man and his smelly pipe have returned to pollute the staffroom. Why could he not have stayed in hospital?'

'Oh, no,' cried Miss Oshodi. She rushed out blushing.

For the first time in his adult life Mr Mobbs was beginning to enjoy himself. His brain surged with power like a 1000 cc motor bike. He did not tremble as 4C burst through the door.

'I still can't find your books, Mobbo,' shouted Jenkins.

'That is because you sold them to a second-hand bookshop.'

'I never.'

'And a word of warning: I should take back the lead you stole last night.'

'I never stole no lead!'

'It is in the back of your shed under a tarpaulin and if I have a word out of you I will ring the police immediately.'

Jenkins slunk into his seat. There was a bubble of excited chatter. 'I should inform your friends in the class, Jenkins, that if there is so much noise as a pin dropping I will shop you immediately.' Jenkins glared round the class. There was complete silence. To Mr Mobbs it felt like swimming in a warm bath. Now, if he spoke to the class, his voice was not absorbed like a sponge but echoed clearly off the walls.

He had the same success with 4D. He was able to meet Wilson at the door and inform him that he knew Wilson had planned to disrupt the class at 10.30 by making everybody bang their desk lids; if this happened he would immediately inform the Head about who had written the graffiti in the school toilets that the Head had raged about in assembly. Apart from whispers of 'How does he know?', the class settled down to work. They were even more impressed when he told Turner not to pass the gum round.

'I ain't got no gum,' said Turner.

Mr Mobbs lifted him up by his shirt collar and took three packets out of his top pocket.

From that day he was treated by staff and pupils with great respect. But he left at the end of the term. He joined the police force as a detective where his rate of detection broke all previous records. He solved three murder mysteries in a year. It became so easy that he tired of it and bought and sold antiques. He was particularly good at auctions. It is said he made half a million. He spent much of his spare time at the races. From chatting to jockeys and trainers he became a successful tipster in a leading newspaper. He provided them with inside information the like of which they had never known from a correspondent before.

When the Headmastership of his old school became vacant, he could not resist applying. The governors did not want to give the job to a racing tipster but he found out their addresses and visited each one in turn. They found out in the course of his visits that he knew a great deal about their private lives. His appointment to the post was a mere formality.

He made a very successful headmaster because he always seemed so well informed about what was going on in every part of his school. Occasionally, he made trips to London. He was seen in Whitehall. It was rumoured he was working for MI5 but he denied this. What do you think?

The Quiet Bully

We went to live in the country during the war. We weren't evacuated or anything like that. No, my Dad rented a smallholding, about fifty acres, and there was a cottage with it. Well, half a cottage anyway. My Mum, Dad and me lived in one half and Madge, Alice and Surrey in the other.

I noticed Madge first. She was a little woman shaped like a milk churn with a fat, blotchy face; she seemed cheerful enough and one day passed me a bag full of conkers over the hedge. I was puzzled about the man we later called Surrey. He seemed to have two jobs. One day I would see him going down his drive dressed in scruffy clothes, carrying a spade or fork; the next day he would be wearing a smart blue uniform, carrying a peaked cap under his arm. The other neighbour did not come out much; she was a long, bony woman with a big head that drooped as she walked. Not that she walked very far. She would shuffle a few paces down the garden in her big blue slippers and that was her lot for the day. She reminded me of a sunflower gone to seed.

About a month after we moved in, Surrey knocked at the door and asked if we wanted any help on the farm for two days a week. He told us that he worked as a chauffeur/gardener for a woman who lived in a big house across the road and that, because of the war, he had to find at least two days a week farming or mining or doing some other 'essential' job.

Things soon picked up on the farm with Surrey about. He could mend anything and organise everything. He was good to me, too. He took me fishing, birds' nesting and catching moles. One day after mole-catching he said he would show me how to skin them; he sold the skins for a shilling each. We went past our end of the cottage, through the gates to Surrey's half. As soon as we shut the gate, Surrey started to tiptoe and I did the same, without understanding why. Only when we were safely in the low shed at the back of the house did Surrey walk normally and talk again.

'Why did we have to be so quiet?' I asked.

'Because the bell hasn't gone yet.'

I had only known Surrey a month and did not want to seem cheeky but I was so puzzled by his answer I could not let it go.

'What bell?'

'The bell for Alice to get up from her after-tea rest.'

'Is Alice that thin one?'

'Yes,' said Surrey, lighting the three candles in bottles so we could see to skin the moles.

'Why have you got two wives?'

'I haven't,' said Surrey and chuckled at the back of his throat – a curious noise that I heard no more than twenty times during the years I knew Surrey; you very seldom saw him smile, let alone laugh.

Mind you, he did not have much to laugh at, I decided, when I found out all about him over the next few weeks. He was married to the milk churn, Madge, and they had been living in the cottage for twelve years. About two years ago, a relative had asked if Surrey and Madge would have her cousin Alice for a fortnight's holiday in the country. Her nerves were very bad and a breath of country air would do her good. Madge and Surrey let her come and she stayed for years. I think it was mainly Surrey's fault; he was too nice a bloke – or too scared. I am not sure which. One thing I am sure of, though, Surrey and Madge could not have wanted her to stay. She was a real pain.

The first time I met her was when I went in with Surrey for a cup of tea; we had been mending the tractor after my Dad had driven it into a gatepost and bent the radiator.

'This is John, from next door, Alice,' said Surrey, after he had wiped his boots about two hundred times on the beet-pulp bags outside the door.

'Hello, dear,' said the wilted sunflower. She put one of her red, bony hands on my head and the other on my arm. I froze – almost literally – because her hands were cold and damp, like a fish feels when you take it off the hook. I hated people touching me, particularly people like Alice.

'How are you?' I asked, taking a step back to disengage myself. It was what my Mum had told me to say if I met anybody.

'Oh, as well as can be expected, in the circumstances, thank you dear,' said this Alice, sighing like a balloon going down. 'Not too bad today, better some days than others, but never very well, I'm afraid.' She smiled a sad martyr's smile.

I had not expected a speech, but it was a speech I was to hear many times in the next ten years, even though I never again made the mistake of asking her how she was.

Anyway, on that first morning, I eventually got my cup of tea. I was told where to sit, and Madge, Alice and Surrey asked me questions about where we lived before. I had only drunk half my tea when a bell on the mantelpiece started to ring. Alice jumped up immediately and bolted out of the room, faster than I had ever seen her move before.

'Has she gone to catch a bus?' I asked.

'No, she's gone to see if she can lose herself.'

Although I had only seen Alice once or twice and spoken to her only once, I already thought it was a good idea if she lost herself.

'She always tries to lose herself about this time,' whispered Madge, stirring the remains of her tea, taking care not to clink the spoon on the side of her cup.

'Has she ever lost herself?' I persisted, not understanding the situation at all.

'Shush,' said Surrey. 'Yes, she sometimes loses herself; but we have to be very quiet.'

When I found that Alice had only gone for a sleep, I was really disappointed. 'Losing yourself' meant losing consciousness and I soon became aware how much Surrey's and Madge's lives depended on Alice's 'losing herself'. She tried to lose herself three times a day, between eleven and half past, one till two, and four till five. The trouble was, even if she lost herself, it wasn't any good. You would think after she had a real good kip she would be a bit more cheerful. Not likely. One day I was in there waiting for Surrey to finish his dinner. Alice had lost herself really well; you could tell from the deep, snoring noises coming out of the front room – she had a bed downstairs. Well, she was so well lost that Surrey and Madge even started a conversation; they usually sat and stared at each other if Alice was kipping.

Suddenly Alice stopped in mid-snore and a moment later came staggering through the door.

'Had a good sleep?' I asked, trying to be friendly.

'Oh, no, dear,' she said with that sad smile. 'I didn't manage to get off.'

'But we heard you snoring.'

'I think you must be mistaken, dear,' she said, her smile thin and icy. 'And even if I do lose myself for a few seconds, I always sleep feverishly. I wake with an appalling headache. Still, we mustn't complain, must we?' she added with a sigh.

I went out with Surrey to mend the barn door. Dad had just

'caught' it with a tractor wheel when he was backing up to load some barley.

'How long is Alice stopping with you?' I asked Surrey while he was trying to wrench the large black nuts off the door.

'Oh, I don't know about that.'

'Do you want her to stay?' It's funny how you dare ask things as a kid that you would avoid later. Surrey avoided me, though.

'She's not well. Her nerves are terrible.'

'Where are her nerves?'

'Ooh, I don't know . . . . pass me that spanner. She's real badly,' said Surrey, fiercely, as if I had asked him another question. 'She doesn't get a wink of sleep most nights.'

'How do you know?'

'Well, she wakes up, making herself drinks and that,' said Surrey, yawning.

I said nothing after that; but I thought a lot. It did not seem to make sense. Poor old Surrey, being woken up by Alice, banging about making herself a bacon sandwich or something, while during the day he had to creep around while she was kipping like a horse. It was not very surprising that Alice did not sleep much at night, what with losing herself three times a day. No, I could not understand it; I would have sent old Alice back where she came from in no time. Why did Surrey and Madge put up with her?

I got some clues two weeks later when we were threshing a wheat stack. Surrey and I were feeding sheaves from the stack on to the threshing drum where my Dad cut the string and fed them into the whirring knives. Bob Lord – big, enormously strong and slow-talking – was carrying the huge sacks of wheat into the barn. Bob left his sacks and came and stood below the stack.

'Hey up,' he shouted. 'Is Surrey up there?'

'Yes,' I shouted back above the noise of the drum.

Bob's drawling voice floated up from the bottom of the ladder. 'I reckon there's someone wants him.'

It was the understatement of the year, as I could see when I went to the other side of the stack. Alice was standing the other side of the gate, between our house and Surrey's. She was waving her arms, flapping about like a chicken without a head and screaming 'Frank' (Surrey's name) so loud you could hear her clearly above the noise of the drum.

The thing I noticed about Surrey as he rushed down the ladder was his face. He had gone red; he was very embarrassed and did not know what the hell to do. Luckily for him though, help was on the way. the advantage of being high up on a stack was that

you could see most of the village. From where I was, for instance,
I could see the quarter past three bus pull up at the corner.
Hardly had the wheels stopped moving when the 'milk churn'
appeared and started running across the field. I had never seen
Madge run before; little legs pumping along, shopping bag and
hair flying in the wind. Inside two minutes, Alice, Madge and
Surrey disappeared into the house. Surrey came out about ten
minutes later but he only grunted when we asked him if
everything was all right so we did not press him.

He told me the next day what had happened. Alice's nerves
were so bad she could not be left by herself so poor Madge was
like a prisoner in her own house. She had to do some shopping
and once a week Madge would catch the quarter past one bus to
town, rush round the shops like someone in a fit, and leap on the
quarter to two bus back home. Yesterday she had missed the bus
and Alice's screaming for Surrey had been the result.

So you can see that Surrey did not have much of a life at home.
As time went on it got worse, particularly the bells. There was a
bell for Alice to go and lose herself, one for her to get up, one for
Madge to start the washing, one to start making the tea, etcetera.
It was like living in a belfry in their house.

One day when I was mending a broken fence with Surrey, a
peculiar thing happened. We had to put in a new fence post; I was
holding it upright and Surrey was driving it in with a crowbar.
I had my eyes shut tight as usual. I was scared of Surrey missing
the post and hitting me on the head and somehow it was not so
likely to happen if I had my eyes shut. Of course, if he had
crowned me with that enormous lump of iron I would never have
opened my eyes again. Anyway, there I was holding the post, eyes
and face screwed up – and nothing happened, no bangs on the
post. I opened my eyes to see what was happening and there was
Surrey flat on his back with the crowbar across his chest. His face
was bluey-white. I was scared. Then his hands and legs started to
twitch; soon he was sitting up.

'What's up, Surrey?'

'Nowt,' he said, quite fiercely for him. 'I just had a funny turn.'
My Dad said he ought to see a doctor. 'Not likely,' said Surrey.
'I've never had a doctor in me life, and I ain't starting now.
There's nothing wrong with me, anyway.'

There was though; his turns got worse. In the end, one day
when the doctor came to see Alice – he came about once a month
– Madge asked him to see Surrey. Surrey was annoyed but he
was also scared of the doctor so he had to sit down to be
examined. The doctor gave him some pills and told him not to do

anything strenuous, like lifting heavy weights. After that he had a look at Surrey every time he came to see Alice. I think it was a change for him to be coming to see Surrey. I don't think he thought much of Alice. Every time my Dad saw him he asked how Alice really was. He usually just grunted, but one day he said that if she was as ill as she thought she was she would have died years ago.

Surrey was carrying a sack of meal to the pigs when he fell down dead. The track to the pigsty was wet and muddy so perhaps he slipped first before his heart attack. I remember clearly what he looked like when my Dad and me found him lying there. He was face down in the mud, his hair was wet as it had started to drizzle and the white pigmeal was all over his hands and body. Lumps of it began to clog together in the wet. The pigs were grunting and squealing for their food. It seemed somehow an awful place to die, although I suppose Surrey had not known much about it.

Everybody was surprised as well as upset by Surrey's death; they should not have been surprised, I know, but Surrey was a person they had all taken for granted. He did most of the work, never complained or caused any trouble. Madge was very upset as you can imagine. She was so bad she had to go and spend a few days with a relative. This left Alice by herself. She had never been left for more than half an hour at a time for years and now there was nobody to cook her meals, set her bells going and stand guard while she lost herself.

The funny thing was that Alice bore up very well. She went to town to do the shopping, fed the chickens, dug the garden and even went to the pictures once or twice. When Madge came back from her visit, Alice looked after her for a change. She took her her meals in bed, cleaned the house and did the washing and shopping.

When Madge got a bit better, Alice's nerves came back. Soon she was in her old routine again, losing herself in the day, banging about at night and running her life by the bells. Things stayed like that for a few years until Madge died.

Again Alice bore up wonderfully well. She seemed to thrive on people dying. Almost six months later, she advertised in the paper for a companion to share the house (she had inherited it from Madge because Surrey and Madge never had any children). She lives with this companion, a Mrs Marshall now; unfortunately though, as soon as Mrs Marshall came, Alice's nerves got bad. Now Mrs Marshall looks after her in the same way Madge used to. I hope Alice bears up all right when Mrs Marshall dies.

HUNGER

Brown had driven the land-rover into the bleak Northern waste
lands as far as it could go. Then he had walked, carrying the light
canvas stretcher. Though fat and wearing a rucksack, he made
his way sure-footedly over the uneven, frozen ground. The
rucksack was almost empty. He had eaten little over the past two
days and was down to the last of his food.

Back in the city old Larsen had warned him about going alone
into the Northland.

'The climate's bad enough,' Larsen had said, 'but there are
some weird things bred in the wilderness. You've heard of the
Abominable Snowman of the Himalayas, the Wendigo of North
America. Well – there are tales of worse creatures than that up
there by the lake. Neither human nor animal. Man-eaters.'

'Trolls,' Brown nodded. 'That's what they call them.'

'Demons, ogres, trolls,' snapped Larsen, scowling at the hint of
a smile on Brown's face. 'Call them what you like. You've heard
the tales about them. They eat people. Some of the tales could be
true.'

Brown, however, had survived in many tight corners of the
world and Nielsen, one of his men, was a fortnight over-due. The
word had been that Nielsen had last been seen near Bogen Lake.
Brown was determined to find him.

He had been trudging for nearly an hour along the shore of
the vast lake before he saw the figure in the distance. As still
as a rock or a beast waiting for its prey, it made no move towards
him.

'My name's Brown,' he called when he was near enough.

The figure only nodded. It was dressed from head to foot in
skins with the fur side outwards.

'I'm looking for someone. Name of Nielsen. Know anything
about him?' Brown asked. The figure nodded again. Its eyes, deep

set in dark hollows, looked Brown over without expression. Its
thick eyebrows and beard did not hide the stark boniness of its
face. That famished look was in odd contrast to its large pot belly.
As Brown came up, it stood with its head tilted slightly
backwards and its large nostrils snuffed the air pig-like. Then it
licked its lips, revealing large yellow teeth and Brown was more
reminded of a wolf.

'Where is Nielsen?' Brown enquired. 'Hurt?'

'Dead.' The voice was deep and hoarse.

'Who are you?'

'Glarak.'

'How did he die?'

'Fell. Broke his neck.'

'Where's the body?'

Glarak turned away and pointed with one furred hand.

'Right.' Brown hitched the stretcher more comfortably on his
shoulder. 'We'll carry him back to the truck and radio in. You'll
be paid. Is it far?'

'Far,' Glarak growled harshly and led the way along the lake
side. Brown followed, feeling a stir of unease.

After they left the lake, the landscape stretched away around
them both, featureless except for where an outcrop of rock or a
deep dip in the ground broke the monotony. Once or twice Glarak
turned his head to check that Brown was still behind him.

'Hang on,' Brown called at last. 'Stop. Let's have a breather
and a snack.' He put the stretcher down and unslung his
rucksack. 'I've got some grub here. Do you want some?'

Glarak hurried back eagerly. Brown sat on a rock, the broken
loaf and the scraps of meat beside him. He felt suddenly cheerful
as he bit into the morsel of bread he had torn off. He liked food.

He was less cheerful as he watched Glarak gobbling and
snorting. He had finished the rest of the bread and all the meat
before Brown could stop him.

'You were hungry,' Brown told him with a shade of bitterness.

'Always.'

'Brown looked round. 'A hungry land,' he observed.

'Hungry,' Glarak snarled.

'Funny thing – hunger,' Brown mused. 'A man will eat
anything if he's hungry. I've been all over the world in my time.
And I've been hungry, like now. Eaten all sorts. Rhino, hippo,
even hyaena in Africa. Polar bear in Greenland. In Australia I
ate witchetty grubs.'

'Witch-witch-,' Glarak's thick tongue stumbled over the
word.

'Like big white maggots,' Brown told him. 'All right if you don't think about them. Savoury, in fact.'

Glarak grunted appreciatively.

''Course, I'm lucky,' Brown went on. 'I'm not squeamish. Far from it. I like experimenting. I'll try anything. Someone once said that I like wild places simply because of the strange foods I find there. Some truth in that. Other people would be put off. Not me. Always ready to try anything new.'

'Human flesh?' purred Glarak, his small eyes gleaming.

'No. No. Certainly not.' Brown was definite, frowning. 'I draw the line at that.'

Glarak grinned, his teeth like a row of tombstones.

'Bad country, this.' Brown changed the subject. 'There have been a lot of disappearances up here in the past six months. Five at least. This will be the sixth.'

'Seventh,' grunted Glarak, still grinning fixedly at Brown. A crafty look crosses his face. He licked his wet lips with relish.

'Strange, in a way, though,' Brown considered. 'There aren't any large wild animals up here. No fast rivers. No cliffs.' He hesitated. 'Something else?'

Glarak got to his feet. 'We go now,' he ordered.

They came to the hollow about half an hour later. It was a deep, steep-sided dip in the ground, lined by sheer faces of rock. At the bottom gleamed a skeleton.

'Bones, eh?' mused Brown. 'Quick work. He's only been missing a fortnight.'

'Birds, animals, insects,' Glarak said quickly.

Brown said nothing as they scrambled down.

When he had gathered up the bones, parcelled them in the stretcher and tied the bundle firmly, he looked up at the rock walls.

'Surprising,' he pondered. 'It's not hard to see the danger. Unless,' he went on, 'he came over the top in the dark.'

'Not dark,' Glarak told him. 'Mist.'

'Mist?'

'It comes down quickly sometimes.' Glarak lifted one furry paw and lowered it slowly to show him how. 'Maybe the man is frightened and starts to hurry. Maybe he hears something behind him. He runs right over the edge and dies.'

He paused. There was something almost gloating about the way he looked at Brown.

'Then he is eaten,' Glarak said.

'By wild animals?'

'Yes.'

Brown was taking a compass bearing for the way back to the land-rover when Glarak shook his head and pointed in another direction.

'Not that way,' he said. 'This way. Easier.'

Brown shrugged. 'If you say so.' He led the way.

Shortly afterwards the mist started to come down. It thickened swiftly. Brown struggled on through the blinding cloud. Its chill sharpened the pangs of hunger he felt. He could hardly hear Glarak's footsteps in the mirk behind him. Then, suddenly, he knew he was alone.

'Glarak!' he called. The blank whiteness returned no echo. He shivered and pressed on, hurrying now.

The abrupt, hideous scream behind him stabbed panic into his brain. He lurched forward, half-running. Then, at his feet, the mist was clearer. He was poised on the rim of a sheer drop. The stretcher slipped from his shoulder and toppled down the rock face, clattering. He struggled to save himself, his arms cart-wheeling but a pebble turned under his foot. He pitched forward.

In the deep hollow the bulky figure had a fire going. The mist had cleared. The stretcher lay against the rock wall where it had fallen. The body, quite dead, lay near it.

'Starving!' the figure mumbled. 'I'm starving!' Carefully it adjusted the two forked sticks, placed ready for a roasting spit, at either side of the fire.

A long knife was being carefully stropped on a stone. The thick coat would not be easy to cut through. It had not been a skin jacket but, as he had expected, body fur. The gloved hands had been, in reality, paws.

Seeing the trap, he had slithered down the rock face, cried out once and then waited in silence. Glarak, hurrying greedily to inspect its prey, had suspected nothing. Three mighty blows with a pointed rock had settled the matter.

Brown whistled quietly as he tested the edge of the knife on his thumb. His fat face shone with pleased expectation.

Never in a long and varied eating career had he tasted troll meat. He was really looking forward to it.

The Wee White Ball

Mr T Hammenburg snarled into the intercom: 'Miss Willis, get Bishop in here immediately!'

He paused from looking at the papers in front of him to light a fat cigar. Smoke billowed round him. Then he went to the window and gazed out over Nettleford, one hand behind his back.

There was a timid knock at the door.

'Come!' ordered Hammenburg, not turning.

A small man stood staring at his back and the smoke halo.'You wanted me, sir?'

'Indeed I wanted you, Bishop. How come we lost the Contra contract?'

'It was a mistake, sir. A mistake with the figures.'

'And who made that mistake, Bishop?' Mr Hammenburg swung round on him.

'I did, sir.' Bishop gazed at the floor.

'Why, Bishop?'

'It was the computer, sir.'

'You are blaming the equipment I so expensively provide?'

'Well, no, sir but...'

'No buts, Bishop. You know what they say about computers: "Rubbish in: rubbish out". I expect 110% efficiency within this firm I built up from nothing. New equipment must be mastered.

'Yes, sir.'

'Let me tell you, Bishop, that I have just taken up the game of golf. I have had one lesson from the professional, one mark you, and I have mastered the swing. I intend to play this afternoon and I shall knock that little white ball around in par or thereabouts because of my application to the task before me. That is why I am such a success in everything I do. Application, Bishop. You have no application and therefore you are fired!'

'Get out!'

Mr T Hammenburg wheeled out his trolley to the first tee of Nettleford Golf and Country Club. It had a large resplendent red hide golf bag on it with nine polished iron clubs and three wooden clubs hidden inside their fur covers and a bronze-headed putter.

He was dressed immaculately for the game complete with an American type sun visor and a white golf glove on his left hand, though the striped pullover did somewhat emphasise his paunch.

He gazed down the fairway of the 410-yard first hole and selected his driver. Then he bent down to tee up the ball on a golden tee his wife had given him.

'Do you wanna game?'

A small Scottish voice interrupted his thoughts of the massive drive he was going to hit.

He looked up. A small pencil-slim girl stood there. She looked about fifteen and was no more than four feet ten inches tall. She carried a shoulder bag with five rusty looking clubs in it.

'Run away, little girl,' he said.

The girl stood her ground. 'It's no gude playing on ya own.'

'Do you know this course then?'

'Och sure.'

'Then you can walk round with me and pull my trolley and spot my ball.'

'I'll give ya a game.'

'Men and women can't compete at this game.'

'Well I'll tell ya what. I'll pull ya trolley and take a swing at the wee ball now and again.'

It was a hot day. Mr T Hammenburg was already perspiring. 'Very well then,' he said.

He stood up to the ball as taught by the professional, waggled the club and then swung back before lunging down on the ball. It shot off the toe of the club and disappeared into a small copse at the side of the fairway.

'Ya didna swing through the ball,' commented the girl. She bent down, teed her ball and then hit it sweetly down the middle of the fairway with no seeming effort.

'Just a little adjustment of the feet needed I think,' he said.

'No ya lunged at it. Ya must swing.' She pulled his trolley towards the copse. 'Come on!'

She found the ball under a bush. 'It's unplayable,' she declared. 'You can drop out with a penalty of one shot.'

'I can hit that,' he said. He selected a seven iron, heaved back and moved the ball one yard. It was now in deep grass. The girl made no comment until he took a five wood for his next shot.

'Ya'll never hit that. Tak your pitching wedge.'

'I can't reach the green with that, he said. He made a massive swing and moved the ball another two yards forward.

'Now will you take your wedge,' she said.

He huffed and puffed and then took his wedge and managed to get the ball back on the fairway. It was now level with the girl's first shot; he had taken four. She played her second shot into the heart of the green some ten feet from the pin. He hit the turf behind the ball with his next shot and then scuttled the next along the ground, over the green behind a small hillock.

'Just a little chip with a nine iron,' said the girl.

'No, I'll cut it up with my sand wedge,' he declared. He swung, caught the ball with the sole of the club and sent it back across the green to where he had previously been on the fairway.

The girl waited patiently as he stalked back. And while he four putted, eventually taking twelve for the hole. She was down in two putts for a four for the hole.

'Just settling in problems,' he declared as they walked towards the second tee.

'Ya'll have a lot of them if you dinna keep ya head doon,' she said.

He ignored her and went to tee his ball first even though etiquette demanded the winner of the previous hole teed up first. This time he swung more slowly. The ball set off straight. 'You see!' he shouted. 'I've got it.' Then the ball took a violent turn until it was going sideways and landed in a deep bunker.

'You've sliced it,' declared the girl. You swung from out to in. Swing from in to out. She then propelled her ball into the middle of the fairway with great ease.

When they reached the bunker he took out his five wood.

'What have ya got that for?' asked the girl.

I can reach the green with it,' he said.

'Don't be a fool. Take your sand wedge.'

'No,' he said. Four shots later and covered in sand from head to foot, he took his sand wedge. He was eventually down in eleven. The girl took five.

The next hole was a short par three over water.

'Seven iron,' said the girl.

'I think I can reach with a nine,' he said. 'I don't want to be over the back.'

He took a nine iron. 'Plop,' went the ball in the water, as did the next two. He eventually took eleven on that hole. The girl holed her putt from a perfect shot for a birdie two.

He got redder and angrier as the round proceeded. No matter how he tried he could not hit the ball straight and true and this young slip of-a-thing could. On the eighteenth fairway as his ninth lost ball disappeared into someone's garden, he let out a squeal of anger. He took the one remaining ball from his bag and aimed straight as the club house windows.

'What are ya at?' enquired the girl.

'Stand back!' he shouted. He hit the ball as hard as he could. It was the only straight shot he had hit all afternoon.

It rose about six feet above the ground and went right through the main lounge window of the club house, brushed the hair of the Club Secretary who was enjoying a quiet whisky and broke a gin bottle before finally demolishing the mirror behind the bar.

The Secretary stormed out. 'I saw that!' he shouted. 'You fool. You imbecile!' By the powers invested in me by the committee I declare that you are expelled immediately. Never set foot on this course again!'

The Professional looked up from repairing a club. 'Did ya have a gud game?' he enquired of his daughter.

'I was four over par,' she said.

'That's gude,' he said. 'Do ya know a Mr Hammenburg has just given me a complete set of clubs, a bag and a trolley. I think they'll suit you nicely, when ya grow up a bit.'

'Is he a fat man with a red face?'

'That's him.'

'He's done a wise thing. His swing was terrible. He couldna master the wee white ball.'

In his office the next day Mr T Hammenburg paced up and down. His red face was now pale. From up there on the twentieth floor of his office building he could see the tall pines that surrounded the thirteenth green. He had spent a restless night. Small white balls had flown about in all directions. Finally he sat. 'Get me Bishop!' he said over the intercom.

'But you fired him yesterday,' said Miss Willis.

'I know I fired him but...' shouted Hammenburg. He stopped. 'I'm sorry I shouted,' he said meekly. 'I know I fired him but get him at his home, please.

Miss Willis sat stunned still holding the receiver. Never in ten years of working for Mr Hammenburg had he apologized to her or said 'please'. This golf game that he had taken up must be doing him good.